Hearts

An Aubrey Stewart Mystery

TO: Jerry (BIL)
Happy Reading
BJGupton.
10-8-14

B J Gupton

BEARHEAD PUBLISHING

- BhP -

Brandenburg, Kentucky

BEARHEADPUBLISHING
- BhP -
Brandenburg, Kentucky
www.bearheadpublishing.com

Hearts
An Aubrey Stewart Mystery
by B J Gupton

Cover Design by Bearhead Publishing

First Printing - September 2014

ISBN: 978-1-937508-31-9
1 2 3 4 5 6 7 8 9

Disclaimer

This book is a work of fiction. The characters, names, places, and incidents are used fictitiously and are a product of the author's imagination. Any resemblance of actual persons, living or dead is entirely coincidental.

Proudly printed in the United States of America.

Hearts

An Aubrey Stewart Mystery

Follow me on Facebook at:
Brenda Joyce Gupton
Contact me at: bj.gupton@yahoo.com

Dedication

This book is dedicated to my Joey.

"But the fruit of the spirit is love, joy, peace, longsuffering, gentleness, goodness, faith, meekness, temperance: against such there is no law." Holy Bible KJV Galatians 5:22-23

Chapter One

As Aubrey entered the darkened Operating Room corridor, a muffled clunky sound, coming from the end of the hall, grabbed her attention. Tracing the sporadic dull thump down the hall to OR Ten, the operating room reserved for emergency heart surgeries, she noticed an empty patient bed, from the Intensive Care Unit, shoved to one side of the hall. The cardiac surgery team would likely be spending the night in an attempt to repair this patient's failing heart.

She peeked through the narrow window positioned above the vertical bar door handle. Two huge lamps flooded the surgical area with light. The rhythmic sound of the heart monitor crossed the room and faintly whispered to Aubrey's keened ear as it recorded each beat of the patient's heart.

Wearing a gown, gloves, and a mask, Mary Beth Owens, Aubrey's longtime friend and colleague, and the circulating nurse on call, appeared to be assisting the surgeon while the anesthesiologist sat perched on a stool directly behind the patient's head. Occasionally, the clang of an instrument hitting the sterile-draped metal tray punctuated the tension that shrouded the room. There was no mistaking that the spare figured man underneath the surgical garb was Dr. Greg Palmer. Not a heart surgeon, but an ear, nose and throat surgeon.

Dr. Palmer wasn't credentialed to perform open heart surgery; however, the room appeared to be set up for opening the chest. Aubrey watched as Mary Beth held a basin over the operative field and Dr. Palmer's gloved hands, covered with blood, appeared above the blue drape. Aubrey caught her breath, backed away from the door, and moved down the hall toward the Recovery Room, each footfall creating an echo in the otherwise silent hallway.

When she had finished her paperwork and entered the post anesthesia charges for the surgical patient she had recovered and taken to the orthopedic unit, Aubrey let out a deep sigh and tossed her patient's PACU record onto the day's stack in the basket situated at the corner of the desk. At least she wouldn't have to hang around to recover the case in OR Ten; all patients from the Intensive Care Unit were transferred directly back to the ICU after surgery.

Still bewildered by that strange snapshot of time she had witnessed, Aubrey wondered what sort of procedure the ENT doctor was busy with back there.

In OR Ten, the rhythm had stopped. A straight, neon green line threaded across the black screen of the cardiac monitor; a red light flashed insistently, but the alarm remained silent, a red X covered that icon. The only person in the room without a mask covering his face, the anesthesiologist, Dr. Ramsey Pate called out the time and turned off the monitor. Mary Beth held a basin over the patient while the surgeon placed a fist sized mass into an icy bath. As she turned away from the surgical field, Mary Beth's eyes remained locked on the burden she cradled in her hands.

Chapter Two

In the locker room, Mary Beth emptied the contents of her chest pocket onto the tower of folded papers on the top shelf of her locker. She then stripped off her blue hospital scrubs and dressed quickly, pausing only for the required struggle with the zipper on her new size six jeans as she tightened her tummy.

On the other side of the room, past a double row of lockers, Aubrey peeled off her scrubs and pulled a sleeveless linen shift over her head. Bending to fasten her sandals, with her dress hiked up and her foot propped on the bench, Aubrey leaned onto her flexed knee and drew her shoulders forward stretching the kinks out of her slender frame. After hearing a locker door slam, she leaned toward the entry to catch sight of Mary Beth, dressed in street clothes and on her way out the door.

Aubrey called out to her, "Hey, you're keeping late hours too. What were you guys doing back there in Ten?"

An astonished Mary Beth twisted her body toward Aubrey while maintaining a tight clamp on the door handle. Ignoring Aubrey's question, she asked sharply, "Why are you still here? All the OR cases ended early. I thought you left at six."

"I had to recover that add-on patient, the open-hip fracture. Dr. Vincent gave the patient his usual, you know, "Nice to the little gray hair," dose of Ketamine to ease her onto the OR table. She didn't rouse for five hours."

Mary Beth's huge brown eyes scanned back and forth across the rows of tall, tan metal lockers. Her head lobbed slightly in an unconvincing nod, her only acknowledgment of Aubrey's reply. Dismissing the temptation to bolt, Mary Beth propped herself against the door frame. Her skinny legs, encased in wheat colored jeans, trembled ever so slightly as she cleared her dry throat to speak.

"The department was closed when I came in, or I would have told you about Dr. Palmer's case. We used OR Ten because a work order to change the bulbs in the overhead lamps had been scheduled for Room Two this evening. Maintenance probably neglected to send out the memo," she said, a strange, mechanical-like restraint in her voice.

Generally, OR Two was the room used for on-call surgeries. Aubrey thought she would have noticed the activity of maintenance personnel in and out of the operating room situated directly across from the short corridor that joined the OR suites with the PACU.

"So, Dr. Palmer just had to do that case before Two could be available. He does seem to enjoy living on the edge." Aubrey said, her blue eyes wide, feigning wonder.

"Look Aubrey, he just wanted to get in and do a quick trach on that kid in ICU, that simple. No policies were violated. Dr. Palmer has every right to operate in there. Heart surgeons don't own this hospital." Mary Beth's wet flaming eyes flitted past Aubrey's gaze before fixing on the floor. "That boy was brain-dead, Aubrey; he had been for a week, so what should it matter."

Aubrey swept a loose strand of blonde hair away from her flushed face and secured the curly lock behind her ear. "Sorry," she offered, then fumbling for a way to change the subject, she asked, "What's that?" as she pointed toward a roll of papers in Mary Beth's hand.

"It's uh, they're just specimen requests. A reminder that I have specimens for Pathology. I better get them dropped off. See you tomorrow." With that, Mary Beth pulled open the door and hurried through, allowing it to close between them.

Standing alone, in the dim locker room tucked deep inside the hospital, countless images flashed wildly through Aubrey's head inciting random recollections. Memories of the procession of all sorts of patients ushered through the operating rooms to have body parts examined, reconstructed, or removed, as life was held in a fragile balance, and the thought that one slip could jeopardize that balance and change a world; of the titillating rumors surrounding after-hours trysts and the stolen naps during the early morning hours by staff members from other departments; and, the most eerie and peculiar event, the remembrance of Dr. Crawford lying across an operating table, dead. Aubrey had not seen the body. She had only heard the story.

The director of the department, Rebecca Krantz, had opened the door to the operating room that morning, nearly two years ago, to discover the body of the female internist sprawled across the table, an empty syringe on the floor beside her. Apparently the doctor had self-injected Sufenta, a narcotic five times more potent than Fentanyl. A single comment, issued by the hospital, had referred to the incident as an unfortunate accident.

Pushing all these morbid images to the farthest corner of her mind, Aubrey slammed her locker door closed. Heading out of the area, she stopped by her desk to grab her backpack.

She turned to leave the Post Anesthesia Care Unit, surveying the quiet area. Empty stretchers neatly lined the perimeter of the unit. Monitors above each station displayed tiny red and green lights that stood out now like miniature Christmas bulbs. The only other lights in the area were the faint red switches of the lights powered by the hospital generator, such a contrast to the usual flurry of activity with doctors and nurses around patients waking from surgery.

At this moment, the world seemed at peace as Aubrey gazed past the empty unit to look out into the night from the third floor. A platinum full moon offered its pale light to the endless Texas sky. Fifteen years she'd spent working in this unit, devoted to patients waking from anesthesia. Thankful that at least her professional life remained in a comfort zone, she locked the double doors to the unit and faced the dark corridor connecting the Post Anesthesia with the Operating Rooms.

Whiffing the slight, stenchy odor made by the surgical cauterizing knife, that familiar hint of burnt flesh which often lingered after having escaped the operating rooms, Aubrey's thoughts drifted back to OR Ten. What she had seen didn't seem to correlate with Mary Beth's explanation, or, for that matter, the blistering comment Mary Beth made about the patient having been brain-dead for a week, 'so what should it matter....' "*No use even trying to figure it out tonight,*" Aubrey thought. She pulled the strap of her backpack further up on her shoulder and walked around to the main hall.

The OR Secretary's office around the corner was never locked. A single fluorescent light mounted under the counter lit only the desktop. Except for a thin shaft of light at the end of the long OR corridor, the entire area reflected a dull mix of shadowy grays.

Aubrey didn't trust the silent black of darkness. In fact, one of the things she missed most since Douglas had left had been the security she had felt with him lying beside her in the deep of night, hearing the regular lub-dub, lub-dub, of his heart beating and his soft, snory breathing. Of course, there were other things she missed; however, this particular memory didn't anger her or drive her to tears.

Jerking back into real time, as the hallway echoed the closing of a distant door, she blinked to erase the vision of Dr. Palmer, his hands buried in surgical drapes. On tiptoes, she leaned over the edge of the desk to grab the telephone.

"Switchboard, this is Rhoda. How may I help you?" The polite, customer-friendly trained voice sang into the receiver from her nook aglow with panels of switches and lights located in the back corner of the Emergency Room Registration area.

"Hello Rhoda, this is Aubrey Stewart. I'm on call for the Recovery Room tonight. Since it's so late, I'm not going to bother with taking a beeper. Call me at home if you need me."

"Sure thing, Aubrey; you have a good night," responded Rhoda. "The ER seems to be quiet, maybe you won't have to come back."

Aubrey quickened her pace as she rounded the corner toward the ICU and the main hall. The automatic doors didn't swing open. Aubrey pushed. The doors had been locked. A shiver sent a spasm across her shoulders. She twisted the bolt clockwise a quarter turn then pushed the door open to a glaring flood of light from the hall. She had to laugh at herself.   What a ditz.   Scared of the dark.

Directly across the wide hall from the double doors, an identical set of double doors opened into the Intensive Care Unit. Aubrey glanced through the tilted slats covering the windows to see the heads and shoulders of staff members as they buzzed around inside the unit.

In the main hall, near the elevators, a small circle of people stood wiping tears and comforting one another. A woman, her head buried in the shoulder of a straight, tall, older man wearing a WWII cap with an Army emblem attached, let out a low, desperate groan. Their world had paused. The remnant of hope, that tenuous, last thread of hope this family and their friends had clung to, had slipped past their grip, evaporated. Aubrey excused herself, nodding as she momentarily locked eyes with one member of the grieving huddle, then passed around them and headed toward the stairwell.

Once outside, Aubrey paused to take in a slow deep breath of still warm, night air. She hesitated, her lungs fully inflated, when she glimpsed the shadowy profile of a man she didn't recognize hand an envelope to Mary Beth. Neither of the two spoke, so far as Aubrey could tell, as they stood at the back of a van parked side-long at the loading dock.

Aubrey stared as the stranger shoved a large box further into the van and closed the doors. He walked around the van and settled himself into the driver's seat, and Mary Beth disappeared around the corner of the dock in the direction of the Same Day Surgery entrance.

Deliberately, Aubrey remained rigid against the brick wall, still and silent as she watched the van back up, turn to the left, and pull away from the loading area. The driver didn't bother to switch the headlights on until he had driven halfway down the block.

The south-facing brick wall pushed its warmth past her flesh and deep into Aubrey's shoulders. Listening to her own breathing as she sucked the heavy air in through parted lips, Aubrey leaned forward before making the effort to step away from the building. She clutched her keys close to her chest and rushed around the building toward her car.

As she unlocked her car, Aubrey scanned the near empty lot for Mary Beth's car. She recognized most of the vehicles: a beat-up red truck belonging to the respiratory therapist who routinely worked nights; a new BMW, the pride of the night charge nurse in the ICU; a sprinkling of ordinary looking cars, which would seem at home in any parking lot; and the tall pickup truck, with huge wheels bearing treads deep enough for a small rodent to nest without the threat of being crushed, the ranch vehicle of the new Emergency Room doctor. It was impossible for him to park the rig in the doctors' lot because the horse trailer, which seemed to be permanently attached, required too much space. Mary Beth's car was nowhere to be seen.

Chapter Three

The car's headlights cast a critical light on the empty drive as Aubrey pulled in from the alley.

As she unlocked the back door and walked in through the brightly lit kitchen, a note, propped against the coffee maker, greeted her. Aubrey studied the yellow legal size sheet of paper that had been folded in half.

Typically, she chose the inside of a teabag envelope or some such leftover paper for writing lists and notes. Douglas didn't seem to care that trees were sacrificed to provide paper for his neatly-penned communications.

As she picked up the portable phone and dialed his number, she finished reading his scripted excuse for not staying with their son.

Douglas arranged time with Eric based on his business schedule. Since Thursday was the most convenient weekday for him, Aubrey ordinarily took call on those days. He had phoned at noon and assured Aubrey he would take Eric to dinner and stay with him for a while. The absence of his car in the driveway hadn't surprised Aubrey.

"Hello."

"Why are you whispering?" Aubrey cradled the phone as she sorted through the array of scattered books and papers on the counter.

"I don't want to wake Kimberly. It's after one o'clock in the morning, Aubrey." Douglas mumbled into the receiver.

"We both know octopuses can't hear," Aubrey chided, adding quickly before Douglas hung up on her, "And I know what time it is. I didn't transfer my patient to the Orthopedic Unit until after midnight. Did Eric get to bed on time? This is finals' week, you know." As she leaned against the kitchen counter, Aubrey lifted the end of her line, a piece of monofilament fishing line she used to practice tying knots. Aspiring to be a fishergirl, she intended to master the process of tying the knots essential for fly-fishing tackle.

"He was brushing his teeth when I left."

She hooked the line around her deft, slender finger and began to turn the short end around the leader, counting silently to five.

"Aubrey, he'll soon be fifteen."

Aubrey brought the knotted short end through the loop in front of her finger. How could Douglas, without sentiment or regret, allow their nuclear family to come undone? She loosened her perfect Clinch knot and repeated the process.

One Saturday, after Eric had left on his bicycle to spend the day with his friend, Gabe, Douglas lugged clothes, shoes, toiletries, some towels and blankets, and his pillow out to his car while Aubrey monitored the cycles on the washer and dryer. Pressing a pair of Eric's jeans flat, she looked out the window to see Douglas propping his golf clubs against the fence.

"I'll have to make another trip for my golf clubs," he said, as he separated his house key from the others on his key chain, and then nudged the single key around the metal ring and off. After she heard the garage door rumble down, Aubrey stood at the counter, staring down at the key. The dryer alarm blared for the second time.

"Let them wrinkle," she had said to the empty house, and retreated to the comfort of a novel from the previous century.

Still, she loved Douglas and sometimes thought she could forgive him. Douglas didn't want her forgiveness. He wanted freedom, as much freedom as the life-sucking arms of this long-armed, long-legged, fifteen years younger than himself octopus would allow. She tossed the crumpled note in the trash can and switched off the light.

Eric lay across his bed, his face toward the stars affixed to the bedroom ceiling, his limbs pointing in all four directions. A soft glow, from the hall light, created an arc of light across his rowdy, dark blond hair. The slight rise and fall of his chest offered the sole indication of life. Aubrey marveled at this flesh of her flesh, this miracle, as she lightly patted a kiss onto the top of his head.

Her once round, happy manatee infant had morphed into a lithe, fourteen-year-old who seldom smiled and almost never initiated a conversation. When he did speak, his voice invariably squeaked. If a monosyllabic response sufficed, he generally didn't offer more. This stoical indifference seemed to be directed toward just about everything that he would have ranted about only six months ago. Would his youth be spent like her own, just a reminder of loss. Aubrey had prayed for so much more for her own child. As easily as the Clinch knots that she so often practiced tying had unwound, Aubrey's family seemed to be unraveling.

Chapter Four

Aubrey stretched her arm across her side of the bed to smooth the coverlet before plumping and arranging a mass of pillows, on edge, against the headboard. The other side of the bed, Douglas's side, remained in ship-shape order. *"Could it be a sign of denial, some kind of hold out, waiting for him to come home?"* Aubrey thought as she stared at the bed.

A confirming glance at the clock proved that pondering the pathology of divorce demanded more time than she had this morning. She needed to get to the hospital. Fast paced Fridays ruled in the OR and, even though the schedule indicated a short day, add-ons could turn the best schedule into a never ending day. Feeling sorry for herself would have to wait.

Eric had polished off the last of his peanut butter toast and was finishing his milk by the time she got back downstairs.

"So, you have your last two finals today?" she asked.

Eric nodded. Then, to Aubrey's surprise, he spoke, with only an occasional crack in his voice.

"Mr. Roberts said our Biology exam will have all multiple choice questions."

"You shouldn't have a problem acing that one." Science was Eric's favorite subject, in part because his Biology teacher, Mr. Roberts, had managed to obtain fetal pigs for the class to dissect, something generally reserved for the higher grades. Eric and his best friend, Gabe, had talked of nothing else for weeks. Then Gabe's dad received a promotion that required a transfer to Austin. Now, Eric moped through his days, finishing the school year alone.

"Dad said he'll take me to Sea World on Saturday, that is, if it's okay with you." Eric told her in the car on the way to school.

The car to her right honked, alerting Aubrey to go ahead and turn. Without chancing a look toward Eric, while all the time praying her own voice wouldn't squeak, she said, "Hey that sounds like a great idea, a good way for you to celebrate after finals."

Two sentences, two full sentences he had spoken this morning. Miracles happen.

Aubrey pulled up into the semicircle drive at the front of the school. "Do you have your lunch money?"

Eric nodded, clumsily raking his mop of curls flat with his hand, a momentary fix.

"Got your key? You don't have band practice." Since the end-of-year band concert the previous Tuesday, his school day now ended an hour earlier; he would arrive home before Aubrey.

"I can use the tree house."

Eric didn't play in it anymore, but the tree house, resting on two huge branches of the ancient spreading mesquite tree in the backyard, served as a part of his secret entrance to the house. From the tree house, he could climb farther up the tree then crawl into the attic of the garage through a hinged window his dad had installed behind the shutter. Once in the attic, he could open the door and take the stairs down to the mudroom. This was the way he entered when he took the shortcut home through the arroyo and up the alley behind the house. It kept his mother from fussing at him about tracking red dirt into the house.

Rambling around in the attic one day, Eric had discovered his bedroom wall backed up to the large attic room above the garage. He cut an opening in the sheet rock on the back wall of his closet and created a secret door. With boards positioned across the rafters, he laid out a walkway to the window. Gabe, the only person Eric had allowed through the secret entrance, had helped him shove all the Christmas decorations and boxes of junk to one side of the new path.

"You'd rather crawl through that window and into a dusty attic than keep up with a key?" Aubrey turned to him with the question, a half smile lightening her face.

Eric's pensive, brown eyes looked past his mother, as he shrugged his shoulders. Tight as a clam, his mouth had snapped closed and without so much as a "Bye, Mom," or "See you, Mom," he untangled his lanky limbs and crawled out of the car, disappearing into the mass of similarly sized and attired youth.

"At least he opened up a bit," Aubrey consoled herself as she pulled away from the school and drove toward the hospital.

Chapter Five

The fenced lot across the street from the back of the hospital provided no ideal place to park. Park in the little shade accessible in the middle of Texas and get bird poop all over the car, or park in the sun and climb into an oven at the end of the day. Aubrey always opted for the far left space on the last row, in the sun. She left her windows cracked open. Rain fell seldom to never in Buena Vista.

While crossing the street, Aubrey spotted Mary Beth making a beeline toward Greg Palmer, as he drove into his reserved space in the doctors' parking lot.

Aubrey gave credit where credit was due and, in her opinion, Dr. Greg Palmer   deserved little. The list of tolerances for this new doctor had become a catalog of quirks. He demanded his own instrument sets for surgery. Of the twelve attending anesthesiologists on staff, he listed only two that he approved of to be assigned to his cases, one of whom happened to be Dr. Ramsey Pate, the future husband of Mary Beth Owens. He insisted specific circulators be scheduled to take call with him and named Mary Beth Owens as one of those. And, again just last Tuesday, due to his negligence to complete charts that had probably been flagged and stuck in front of him more than once, he forced patients and staff to accommodate his lack of regard for policy.

Two operating rooms had posted several short pediatric ENT cases. The PACU staff geared up for a fast-paced morning of toddlers. The start time for Dr. Palmer's room was delayed more than an hour so that he could go down to the Medical Records Department on the first floor and sign off on charts. Dr. Greg Palmer considered himself above reproach.

For some time, Aubrey had made allowances for him; the pressures of setting up a new practice, the unfamiliar routines of a private hospital, which were often different from those of a large teaching facility, and the tension of being the new surgeon in the OR. After kindness and encouragement had failed, she reluctantly treated him with a cool professionalism. Whenever he gave verbal orders in the PACU, Aubrey responded by immediately placing the chart in front of him so that he could scrawl his illegible autograph. This forced compliance led him to call Aubrey by her middle name, Catherine, frequently prefaced by 'Saint.'

Aubrey couldn't understand why Mary Beth chose to work with the likes of him. She knew him to be a competent surgeon, but certainly nothing stellar. Recalling the procedure she had witnessed the previous night, she thought out loud, "What on earth was that guy up to?" Granted, she had worked fourteen hours and had been exhausted, but the scene she had observed had to have been more than a tracheotomy.

Chapter Six

Across the parking lot, Greg had stepped out of his trophy car, a sleek black Mercedes-Benz S600. He had always had a passion for sports cars and didn't have to wait until he had finished his residency as an ear, nose, and throat specialist to fulfill his dreams. He simply used his potential income and mentioned his father-in-law's name. His "driving around in a crate days" were over.

Through his teen years, Greg's mother had used the allotment his dad sent every month to provide a home for Greg and a wardrobe for herself. When he walked across the sunny, outdoor stage, clutching his high school diploma under his arm, his mother met him with a hug, announcing her intentions to relocate to Las Vegas with her newest admirer, and that Greg could take up the lease on the apartment if he wanted, or he could request the leasing agent allow him to move to a smaller unit. From his dad, Greg received a congratulatory card with a crisp, new Hundred Dollar Bill taped inside.

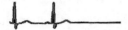

As an undergrad, any time not spent studying, he had worked for a caterer, setting up and waiting tables. He walked or rode his bicycle wherever he went, until he scraped together enough cash for a used Datsun. The car spent more time in the shop than on the street in front of the apartment he shared with a couple of students from Texas. Had it not been for student loans he would never have been able to have finished medical school.

The Mercedes-Benz salesman had said, "Having something to drive that isn't going to depreciate, a classic, why it's an investment you can touch every day. That's better than money in the bank.

"Look at it as an asset. A low-production vehicle like this one will only go up in value," he'd said.

Greg stroked the soft, smooth leather of the seat as he reached for his briefcase.

"Dr. Palmer, wait up," Mary Beth called out as she waved to him.

"Oh, hi," Greg answered. He stood there trapped, with the open car door between Mary Beth and himself, his tanned, lean face grimacing as he faced the sun.

"I'm glad I saw you." She pushed a coppery strand of hair away from her forehead as she approached him. Mary Beth hesitated before continuing, measuring her words.

"I just can't help but have second thoughts about last night, you know, about it being the right thing to do."

With his grip tightening on the handle of his briefcase, Greg exhaled, puffing out a bolus of hot air. He felt like kicking himself for stopping to acknowledge her. He didn't have any patience, especially this morning, for tolerating her whining. "Mary Beth, it's finished. We don't need to think about it ever again. Furthermore, you didn't seem to have second thoughts about the check for ten grand you took home," Greg snapped. Ramsey had said Mary Beth could be trusted to keep quiet.

Ramsey had approached Mary Beth on the evening they had met with their wedding planner. "We ignore the parents' refusal; that's all," Ramsey had told her. Then, he told Mary Beth how much she would receive for a few of hours of her time. "Plus, you'll save three lives." He had made it seem like such a good idea.

After the fact, she doubted her decision. Mary Beth had witnessed patients die before, some of them on the operating table; but, she had never walked away with the feeling she had done less than every thing possible to preserve life.

"It seems like we've been so deceptive."

Biting the inside corner of his mouth, he hesitated before speaking, "What we did was take the burden of making an unpleasant decision off the shoulders of his parents." He lowered his voice, leaned toward Mary Beth and continued, "Every time the ventilator gave that kid a breath, his parents felt responsible; responsible, because they had bought him the car that caused all this. Twelve times a minute they were reminded he was never going to wake up. Twelve times a minute they blamed themselves. Mary Beth, those poor parents didn't need to continue their vigil until we pulled the plug. Haven't they endured enough misery?"

Mary Beth's shoulders collapsed with the weight of Dr. Palmer's words.

"A day, maybe two, that was all he had left. We didn't do anything wrong. He coded while being trached. It happens. That's why the surgical permit plainly states "potential complications, including death." You know that. You've signed as a witness to the signatures on thousands of those documents.

"Let his parents focus on the fact he died during a procedure rather than as a result of driving too fast. Protective, not deceptive. We protected them from having to make the final decision to unplug the ventilator," Greg said.

Groping for a civil way to put an end to Mary Beth's complaining, he added, "Let me get with Ramsey. We'll all get together tomorrow night, have a few drinks and talk it through, okay? It'll make you feel better."

Then, as he nodded toward the far end of the parking lot, he said, "Smile, here comes your sainted sister. Now, I better get going before I get accused of trying to take you away from Ramsey," he announced, looking past Aubrey.

He pushed himself around the car door, carefully sealing the door closed as he pressed the lock button on the key fob, and then tried to distance himself from Mary Beth.

"Dr. Palmer," Aubrey kindly acknowledged him, flashing a polite, millisecond grin in his direction. She thought, *"He would spontaneously combust if he knew I saw him in OR Ten last night."*

Greg responded to Aubrey's greeting with a less than enthusiastic wave.

Mary Beth squinted toward the morning sun, her brown eyes hidden behind mascaraed lashes, as she watched Aubrey approach.

What Aubrey thought she had seen the night before laced with the explanation Mary Beth had given her and tangled all her thoughts. She planned to investigate Mary Beth's story without making waves.

Hooking her arm through Mary Beth's, she lifted her knee in a mock march, "Come on, it's Friday. If we're lucky, our weekend will start in exactly eight hours. Let's get in there and get this day knocked out."

Mary Beth forced an anemic smile and obediently joined her.

Chapter Seven

Mitchell Hughes, by looks the persona of a bodyguard, a towering frame holding blocky, square shoulders and upper arms of the size requiring custom tailored suits, had stepped into the building's lobby and scanned the listing of tenants. "Medical Specialty Consultants" engraved on a brass placard directed him to Suite 509.

A large brown envelope addressed to Mitchell had been placed on the receptionist's desk with a note from the secretary stating she had been called away from her desk and any information he required could be found inside the envelope. A letter of approval for the position, based on his application and background check, topped several pages of material detailing company car and phone use and his obligations as a security specialist. Attached to the last page of the contract, he found a check for his expenses and an advance. Obviously, his resume, embellished in some areas and the deliberate omission of requisite data in others, had done the trick.

Mitchell returned everything to the brown envelope and tucked it deep inside his messenger bag. As he had reached for the door, Mitchell noticed the light of a security camera cleverly positioned behind a potted tree.

Two years and dozens of assignments later, he still hadn't had personal contact with a superior. The orders Mitchell had received from the group for this particular job had been: to relay phone messages to Vince, the guy he had dispatched to the hospital for the pickup of the organs from a nurse Owens; to place listening devices in Greg Palmer's car and in his office; and, to maintain surveillance of the doctor. Mitchell hadn't been told who monitored Dr. Palmer's conversations.

The previous morning Mitchell had watched as Greg said goodbye to his wife and children. They made several trips from the open garage to Leah's parents' white Suburban parked in the drive. Two car seats were placed in the back seat. Greg crammed several pieces of luggage in the back, along with a striped beach umbrella and a big red wagon, while two little girls ran around the drive chasing each other.

Greg had scooped the children up into his arms as they rounded the vehicle and held them both close for hugs before he secured them in their car seats, while Leah's parents situated themselves in the front seat. He followed his wife to the passenger side rear seat and opened the door for her. She leaned up on tiptoes and gave him a quick peck on the cheek before climbing in beside the children. The little girls waved and blew kisses, as Greg closed his wife's door.

Mitchell swallowed the last of his coffee and watched as the tan, taut-muscled doctor backed his black Mercedes out of the garage and turned onto the street, Mitchell cranked the ignition of his rental car and put it in gear. Following Dr. Palmer to the hospital, Mitchell lagged behind a couple of cars and kept pace with the morning traffic.

Mitchell witnessed a brief conversation between Dr. Palmer and Mrs. Owens at the hospital parking lot. Minutes later, the phone rang. New orders came through. This job had been completed last night, or so Mitchell had thought; but apparently, something said by Dr. Palmer or Mrs. Owens had not been received well by the group. The blunder weighted sufficient magnitude to warrant close scrutiny for awhile.

Dr. Palmer struck Mitchell as the type who would want the secret of the harvest buried, and, at this point, the doctor had more to lose than anyone else. As an added assurance or threat, however it might be perceived, the operative agent might be someone Dr. Palmer interacted with daily at the hospital.

Mitchell received instructions to continue the surveillance of Dr. Greg Palmer and to discover the identity of the woman walking into the hospital with Mrs. Owens. He also took a message for Vince, the courier who had made the pick up after the harvest.

As the fluorescent-orange sun glared hot, lifting itself higher off the horizon, the activity of the group surged with new momentum. Mitchell moved his car farther down the street and parked in the shade of a building before calling Vince.

Chapter Eight

Vince grabbed for the phone on the second ring. Mitchell instructed him to call Greg Palmer and thank him. Mitchell could be curt, even arrogant, and it seemed he always wanted to be one step ahead in the game. Vince imagined him to be an ex-Marine or from a military school. The one thing Mitchell never did was joke around, and this new set of orders sounded like some kind of sick joke. He sat up on the side of his bed, his fingers grinding at the right temple area of his head, as he got fully awake.

"Thank him. What am I supposed to thank him for?" Vince asked, with the usual grit in his voice. He and Dillon had left Buena Vista after the delivery. By the time he got back to San Jacinto it was nearly five in the morning. He hadn't had three hours sleep and those guys wanted him to make a social call.

"Just say thanks. Detailed orders will be in your box tomorrow morning. Be sure to check it early." Mitchell ordered.

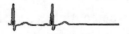

The group carried out every detail of its operation like a covert military sting. Nothing was left to chance. At the time he had found out he had been hired, Vince had received a one paragraph instructional notice and a key to a post office box. A call for a job would come with directions or information. The mail box assigned to him would have supplies, further instructions, and a picture, or detailed description, of the person he was to meet. He knew the name of one person in the group, Mitchell, the contact with whom he communicated. Any other persons he dealt with were there merely for the exchange and there had been no need for introductions.

Vince suspected Manny, the person he had spoken to at the Mercedes-Benz dealership where he had taken his mother's car in for service, to be a member of the group; he had no way of being positive. Manny had struck up a conversation with him, and soon, the talk had turned to Vince's failed attempts to be admitted to medical school. It seemed a little odd to Vince that within days of having talked with Manny an application came in the mail with a letter stating it was being sent in response to his inquiry for the position as courier for Medical Specialty Consultants. Manny probably wasn't a party to the intel of the group, Vince figured; just a head hunter, somebody who could spot the kind of guy who liked to stay under the radar. Vince had hired Dillon, a young man he knew from the all-night diner he frequented, to help with the long-haul driving.

A thank you from this group would carry a hefty price tag. For some reason, they wanted to keep Palmer looking over his shoulder.

Vince could hear the impatience in Mitchell's heavy breath, "I'll call," he said to Mitchell and hung up.

Chapter Nine

The scheduled surgical patients had come and gone without event and several of the nurses had left for the day. Aubrey's interest diverted back to her immediate concern, the case from the previous night. None of it made sense. Not one to inconvenience himself, Dr. Palmer would have added the trach onto Friday's schedule without a second thought, rather than operate in the middle of the night.

Because there shouldn't be anything to send to pathology with a simple tracheotomy, Aubrey decided to find out the origin of the specimen that Mary Beth had taken down for analysis.

In all her years at Blakely, Aubrey had called Pathology only a handful of times. "Hello, this is Aubrey in the PACU, would you mind to check your log to see if a specimen came down from surgery last night around midnight, maybe a little after?" The entry level lab tech eagerly responded to the request. After several minutes of elevator music, there was a second of silence before she heard the lab tech's voice, "Nothing from surgery yesterday evening after six, there were several clocked in before then; but nothing is posted from that time until after eight this morning."

"If a specimen is sent to an outside lab, would you have any way of knowing?"

"Oh yeah, we record everything and track it with the patient's Medical Record Number and an additional number the lab assigns with the forwarding paperwork."

"Thanks for your help," Aubrey said.

"No problem. We do this every day."

Next, Aubrey checked with Maintenance. A work order to change the overhead bulbs in OR Two did exist. Since it had been sent late in the afternoon and not marked as urgent, no immediate action had been taken.

Mary Beth had lied to her. Maybe not about the request for the lights to be changed, but certainly about the specimens. *"But why?"* Aubrey wondered.

Both Mary Beth and Aubrey had been hired to work at Blakely about the same time; Aubrey as a new graduate, and Mary Beth, from the same local university, but with two years' experience as an operating room circulating nurse for the heart transplant team at a large teaching facility in Houston. Her daughter, Cassie, was a year older than Eric. Mary Beth didn't have it in her to be dishonest.

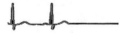

An explanation was overdue. Aubrey tucked her wild blonde mane into a blue disposable cap and left the PACU.

From the hallway, she heard the whispered, deliberate tones of Rebecca Krantz, the OR Director. Dr. Palmer stood in the doorway of the Director's office, his back to the hall. Aubrey watched as he moved further into Rebecca's office and closed the door.

Flanked by rows of operating rooms on either side, with shelves of sterile-packaged instruments and supplies situated at the back, the inner corridor was considered a clean area. As required, anyone entering the area wore scrubs, and head and shoe covers.

"Is Mary Beth around?" Aubrey asked the nurse manning the desk.

"She's in ICU with the case that went direct about thirty minutes ago. You might as well leave a note because Dr. Moore has ordered packed cells and platelets; they're going to reopen. Unless it's really important." The nurse added this last quip in case Aubrey thought her own issue might be a larger concern than a post op bleed.

Aubrey didn't intend to leave a note. "It'll keep until I see her," she said and headed back to the PACU.

Chapter Ten

After stopping off at home for her son and their fishing gear, Aubrey merged her car into the Friday afternoon parade of those trailering jet skis and boats, all of them anxious to relax. She and Eric had enrolled in a series of fly tying and fishing lessons at the lake property owned by the local university.

Blazing into her class, Aubrey offered apologies to her instructor as she unpacked her fly tying kit. "Hello," she whispered to her classmate, as she took her customary place on the wooden bench beside him.

"You're late," the judge muttered, a grin and a wink tacked on to moderate the chastisement.

Half an hour later, Aubrey couldn't get the thread wound tightly enough around the tail of her fly. Most of the others had finished already and were comparing techniques. The judge, with his bent, arthritic fingers was applying body cement to his Woolly Worm fly.

"Too much caffeine today?" the judge asked, nodding toward Aubrey's near naked hook.

"Maybe I need more. Actually, I'm bringing too much work home, or too many work related issues."

"I've been guilty of that more than a few times." He unfoiled a chocolate covered mint and stuck the candy his mouth, then pushed a couple of the green-wrapped treats toward Aubrey.

The instructor came around to Aubrey's hook and checked her spool, reminding her of the ease of tightening if several loops are made before pulling tension. She reconnected her thoughts and selected a yellow strip of chenille for the fly's body.

"Sorry, Judge. I'm not good company today," Aubrey said. She loosened the vise from its perpendicular position in the little wooden box, pushed an eraser over the hook and placed the tools back in the box. Her Yellow Fly wouldn't get finished today. After snapping the box closed, she lifted her backpack and dropped the box inside.

In the shade of the lodge, Aubrey sat on a bench facing the lake and watched as Eric practiced his casting. The judge ambled down the rock path toward her. He doffed his hat, exposing a shock of graying hair, then grunted as he parked himself on the other end of the bench. "So, why was the best fly tier in the class all thumbs today?"

Smiling, she whirled her face toward him, "With only one week left, I didn't want to make all of you guys look bad." Their class, which had started with twelve members, had dwindled in size as the weeks passed. Aubrey was the remaining female among four men; Bob, a diesel mechanic who openly admired her Benz's turbo diesel engine; loud mouth Roger; Jeff, a retired Air Force Captain; and Judge, the geriatric version of Brad Pitt.

"Actually, an incident at work stays in my head; it keeps gnawing at me, wanting me to look at it, do something." Before she left the hospital, Aubrey had filed a Patient Occurrence Memo, reporting what she had witnessed. It wasn't much, but it might invite a look at Dr. Palmer's shenanigans. Reporting the incident hadn't eased her mind a bit.

An idea struck her. "Hypothetically, you've probably heard that word often enough, if I were to ask a hypothetical question about whether something is legal…."

"Whoa!" Judge held his hands out. "I'm just a worn out old rancher. I got tagged 'Judge' years ago when I started judging Rambouillet sheep at stock shows. If you want to know the standards for a champion ram or ewe, the staple length of fleece, any of that stuff, I'm your man. I know land, livestock, and liquor. Law is one L I don't know much about. Anything else, call me and I'll help." He handed Aubrey a business card.

Aubrey took the card and shrugged, "So much for free advice, John Mason." Then, looking him in the eye, she smiled and added, "Thanks, Mr. Mason."

Chapter Eleven

Mrs. Leland, Aubrey's alley neighbor, appeared from her back yard, greeting Aubrey as she pulled into the driveway from the alley, her little dachshund, Malcolm prancing beside her, the tags on his collar jingling. Malcolm and irises were Mrs. Leland's life. Having Aubrey for a neighbor offered another interest. She had appointed herself Aubrey's surrogate mother.

"Look at yourself, thin as a reed. You're not eating enough," she would say. Or, "Be sure to lock the doors and don't leave that back gate open. There's no telling who might wander in here and rob you blind while you're at work. Worse yet, walk right in on you and do God only knows what. You can't be too careful."

Aubrey accepted her neighbor's motherly advice, which was tempered with genuine affection without protest, since her own mother had died before Aubrey's thirteenth birthday.

Ambulance lights had flashed and sirens had blasted when Aubrey's mother had been taken to the hospital late that October night. Aubrey had squeezed her mother's cold, pale hand, even wrapped the slender fingers around her own and tried to push; her mother didn't squeeze back. Aubrey stared at oxygen mask covering her mother's gray face as she lay on the gurney, being wheeled from the house out into the chilled, windy, blackness, by two uniformed EMTs. This had been the last time she had seen her mother alive. She had never known her dad. He had abandoned the family before Aubrey was born.

As they stood in the shade of Aubrey's garage, Mrs. Leland's concern for the day seemed to focus on Eric and her short visit with him the previous afternoon.

"That child is growing up before my eyes. He's lost since Gabe moved off and left him. Those two, now they were thicker than thieves; where you saw one, you saw the other. Yesterday, I watched him as he sauntered up the alley. He stopped by here long enough to grab a couple of my tea cakes, said his dad was picking him up. That's all he said. I swear getting him to talk is like cranking an old ice cream maker the way we used to do, on hot days like today, when I was young and growing up on the farm. Keep turning that old crank long enough and finally, you'd have yourself some ice cream." Mrs. Leland's voiced trailed off with her thoughts.

Then she bounced back to real-time, "He's just lonesome, for Gabe and his daddy. It wasn't until after five that I caught a glimpse of Douglas and that new lady friend of his drive up."

"This morning he actually made conversation, not enough to be labeled a chatterbox, but we did have a dialogue," Aubrey shared, as she grabbed hold of the strap on her backpack. "I think he might be adjusting to the fact that Gabe has moved, or maybe he's getting excited about school being out and that fishing trip with my brother. I watched him for awhile today, and his fly casting is beautiful. In fact, he stayed out at the lake. I'm going to take him a clean shirt to change into for dinner. How about you? Will you be ready in another half hour?" Aubrey asked.

"Indeed I will. Our Friday night fish fry at the Elks Lodge is the highlight of my week. If my doctor ever tells me I have to cut out the fried foods, I'm going to insist he make a Friday exception for that fish. Otherwise, I'll have to draw the line on following his orders."

Mrs. Leland handed her a container of cookies, "For your tea this weekend."

Then she added, "Now Aubrey, you know I'm never doing anything that I can't put down and come over here in an instant. Anytime you need me to take care of that boy, you let me know."

"Thanks, for always looking out for Eric and me. I'll meet you back here in a minute," Aubrey said and went inside to deposit her tea cakes on the kitchen counter and grab a clean shirt for Eric.

Mrs. Leland's endearing qualities had drawn Aubrey to her and seemed to have had the opposite effect on Douglas. He had always taken Mrs. Leland to be a busybody, especially after Mrs. Leland had told them about the lawyer who lived two doors away, on the same side of the street as herself. According to Mrs. Leland, he walked around in his living room stark naked. She knew this because her neighbor across the street, in the house facing the lawyer's, said she saw him almost every morning. These elderly women had diagnosed him as a psycho. Douglas insisted Mrs. Willard probably waited every morning to see if their lawyer neighbor would dash past the open window.

"Some neighborhood watch dogs they are. Would you want some innocent act of yours to be sensationalized and turned into a hot topic at these old ladies next bridge party?" he had asked Aubrey, not expecting an answer.

Aubrey had scowled at him for this mean tirade, convinced that the conversations of Mrs. Leland and her friends were totally harmless. In fact, she rather enjoyed the motherly attention.

The instant Mrs. Leland heard her neighbor's garage door going down, she fastened her back gate and hobbled down the drive to meet Aubrey.

Chapter Twelve

Saturday morning Eric bounded down the stairs, dressed and ready for his dad's arrival. Douglas had made good on his plan for a trip to Sea World.

"I can stay home," he offered, putting the brakes on his excitement as he realized his mother would not be going. The previous trip to Sea World had included both of his parents and Gabe.

"Since when does staying at home and cleaning your room take precedence over a trip to San Jacinto and a chance to ride that new roller coaster? You must be sick! They're advertising The Great White as the thrill of a lifetime!" Aubrey placed her hand on her son's forehead, as if checking for a fever, then tousled his hair. She caught a flicker of light in his eyes as he twisted his baseball cap on.

Waving to Eric from the front door, she stood there in her oldest shorts and the faded T-shirt she had worn in a benefit run several years before. The octopus, impersonating an animated ad for a complete line of makeup, delicately waved her pink, perfect, four inch long claws as Douglas pulled away from the curb. By Aubrey's calculations, the T-shirt she wore was nearly as old as the octopus.

She poured herself a second cup of coffee and walked out onto the patio adjacent to the breakfast room and settled into a chair. This house had not been one the realtor had selected for them to see. Aubrey had spotted the sign in the front yard of the old white limestone house from the corner of Highland. It had been love at first sight. The first floor contained the public rooms. The living room and formal dining room were on the west side of the foyer and grand staircase. A den and breakfast room occupied the east side. The galley style kitchen was perfectly situated for serving both dining areas. Behind the kitchen, a tiny closet staircase separated the mud room and the laundry room. Three bedroom suites and a lounge filled the second floor. From the master suite, a balcony looked out over the well-manicured back yard. Aubrey and Douglas had fallen in love with the uniqueness of the custom-built house, with its light golden hardwood floors, high ceilings, transoms over the doors, and its charming white stone exterior. Visible fossils in the stones, marking eons of time, fascinated Aubrey. The entire house held such a feeling of permanence. It was home. The kind of home Aubrey had dreamed of since she was a little girl. Not the white stone or the house itself, but the feeling that stirred her heart when she saw it, as if she belonged here.

Unlike her grandparents' house. There Aubrey had shared the expansive second floor with her mother, and her sister and brother, Anna and Jack. When their mother had died, Anna had already completed two years of college, and Jack had begun his senior year of high school. Aubrey had spent four years alone upstairs as the ghost of her grandparents' daughter, dreaming of the home and family she would have someday.

Today, she had the entire day to play in her yard. Whenever her spirit needed resuscitation, Aubrey spent time in the red Texas dirt, digging and loosening clots of hard-pack from around the roses and shrubs; planting flowers, preferably native perennials; and pulling weeds. This communion with God's earth was the balm that covered the sadness she so often experienced as a nurse, and the flowers and roses she grew resembled banners of joy and hope.

She took special pleasure in her roses. The Lady Banks' Yellow Rose against the back fence had been a solid yellow blanket for Easter. The blooms only last for a few weeks in spring, and the last dried, faded blooms had fallen to the ground. The cascading branches blanketed the fence with green for most of the year. Aubrey grabbed her pruning shears and commenced cutting older canes and taming the huge bush.

Thoughts of Mary Beth's predicament kept nagging Aubrey. The peculiar incident she had witnessed Thursday night kept winding through her mind. She didn't have an opportunity to talk with her at work on Friday. Mary Beth had called her last evening and left a message. By the time Aubrey arrived home and noticed the message, it was too late to return the call.

Dead branches and leaf trash filled the old wooden wheel barrow. Aubrey pushed the load down the drive and dumped it into the garbage can in the alley. After raking the last of the loose litter up from that side of the yard, she removed her gloves and went inside to return Mary Beth's call from last evening. When Mary Beth's voice did come on, it was a recorded message.

"Hi, Mary Beth. It's Aubrey. Give me call. Maybe we can have dinner," Aubrey spoke to the answering machine then placed the kitchen phone back in the cradle.

Aubrey picked a perfect 'Peace' rose blossom with pink edging, which fades to palest pink mingled with faint yellow. She breathed in a long whiff of the sweet aroma of the rose.

Douglas had purchased it for her at a nursery on the far north end of Highland Street after the TV news channels flashed reports of the end of Desert Storm.

The rose had received the name 'Peace' fifty years earlier. Supposedly it had been shipped out of France by plane just before the German invasion. Half a century later, the rose remained popular for its history and its beauty. Douglas had helped her that February day, as much as he despised gardening, to plant their symbol of hope for world peace.

Aubrey had a cutting from the bush in the kitchen window, hoping for it to take root and make a new plant.

The sound of the telephone ringing interrupted her thoughts. At the door, Aubrey kicked off her clogs and rushed to answer before the answering machine activated.

"Hello," she said, breathless, as she grabbed for the telephone with her ungloved hand, welcoming the return greeting of her friend's voice, though flat to her ear.

Mary Beth's words sounded weighted with sadness. "Sorry I didn't get back to you right away. I slept in today." She clutched the tablet she had planned to use to write a letter to Aubrey, a letter describing the secret lie in her life.

All thoughts of how she would admit the events offered no solace for Mary Beth; she sat, turning the pen end on end through her thumb and index finger, struggling to find words to explain her actions to Aubrey, a person who could not conceive of deception on any level. A straightforward clarifying comment about her participation in the harvest seemed more like an attempt at justification for a sin rather than what she intended. While listening to Aubrey, she crumbled the note, unwritten save Aubrey's name, and tossed it into the trash. Somehow, the actualities and details had to be avoided. Surrendering to the accumulation of stale air trapped in her lungs, she exhaled while Aubrey prattled on about dinner.

"I've been worried about you. Let's get together and have dinner. Eric is with Douglas. We can talk without interruption. How about the River Pearl?" she suggested, referring to a cozy restaurant nestled between and Irish-style pub and a dress shop, in a strip mall nearby. The intoxicating aroma of their homemade bread possessed the power to cause the staunchest dieter to crater. They provided take away meals Monday through Thursday. Friday and

Saturday were the only days the restaurant offered in house dining for lunch and dinner. Aubrey could taste the grilled trout as she spoke. "If I hop in the shower now, we can beat the crowd."

"I'm sorry Aubrey, but I'm supposed to be at Ramsey's for drinks at six-thirty. He's already made a reservation at the club for dinner. Why don't you come over tomorrow after church? Bring Eric. Cassie's spending the night with a friend. She should be home by noon. She and Eric can hang out while we talk. I'll make you an omelet."

One more day wouldn't matter. Aubrey's strategy to discover exactly what had transpired in the operating room had flopped. She would insist on a full accounting from Mary Beth tomorrow.

The one time Aubrey had mentioned her concerns about Mary Beth's relationship with Ramsey, Douglas had said she was jealous.

"I most certainly am not," she said, adamantly. "Everyone knows that a marriage to Ramsey Pate comes with a prenuptial agreement and a five year life, at best. That man abstains from one thing only, faithfulness."

Too many women before Mary Beth had fallen victim to his spell. Aubrey wasn't jealous; she merely wanted to protect her friend from getting hurt. Not that Mary Beth had asked for any help. She had fallen so deeply in love with Ramsey that she didn't even notice his thick glasses, always on the lookout for the next Mrs. Pate.

"That's not jealousy, that's reality. Anyway, how would you know? A man who dates an octopus is too wrapped up to spot jealousy. Kimberly has you blinded with that ink she spits on you,"

Aubrey had flared her fingers toward Douglas, hissing all the while.

When she hung up the telephone, Aubrey thought she knew something of how Eric felt. Lonely. Her friend had not moved out of town, yet a distance definitely existed. A wider gulf than a mere relationship, with a new, almost-husband would cause. Her two other friends, those with whom Aubrey maintained closest ties, were attending a retreat in San Saba. Barbara and Karen wouldn't be home until Tuesday.

Since she had no plans for dinner, Aubrey decided to forage in the refrigerator for leftovers, and after eating, she gave herself a manicure and a pedicure.

She sat with her back propped against pillows on the sofa, toes splayed, their wet glistening nails flared, sipping a glass of wine, engrossed in a movie, when a shadow of light moved across the den wall. Without turning her head, she cut her eyes toward the open window to see a car as it inched its way from the cul de sac. Someone probably lost, checking all the house numbers. The soundtrack of the movie picked up in tempo redirecting her attention to the TV screen.

Licking her finger, then lightly touching a toenail, Aubrey determined her nails dry enough to remove the cotton balls she had stuffed between her toes. Tossing the fluffy white clouds of cotton into the trash, a vision, like a beam of light piercing through a dark sky, tore through her mind; Mary Beth, her expression blank with empty eyes, holding her cupped hands out toward Aubrey.

Chapter Thirteen

Since he didn't want to be concerned that someone might later recognize him and recall having seen him in the hospital, Mitchell hadn't gone inside to ask about the lady he needed to ID. Instead, he waited until he could safely enter Mrs. Owens's house. After Mary Beth had left on Saturday, Mitchell parked down the street from her house. He walked past an elementary school and into her backyard without being noticed. Inside the six-foot wooden privacy fence, he found the French doors unlocked. He noticed the red light by the telephone and pushed it, listening to the messages. They all had been from the same person, Aubrey. Mitchell then glanced through the address book beside the phone and mouthed a silent oath of relief when he found 'Aubrey Stewart.' He jotted down her telephone number and address.

With this information tucked safely inside his chest pocket, Mitchell eased down the hall and to the right, where he found Mrs. Owens's bedroom. He stood in front of the large triple dresser and stared at his reflection in the mirror. His focus drifted from himself to the pale blue robe slung over the chair in the corner of the room, the same blue color as his mother's silk robe.

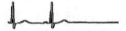

The silk robe he had felt against his cheek while he clung to her, his skinny, six-year-old arms wrapped around her legs. "You'll learn to quit making a sissy out of that boy," his father had screamed as he jerked Mitchell away and ordered him to his room. Mitchell's face tensed as he remembered looking back to see his father's hand striking his mother across the face. After that day, sadness became the only emotion that registered in his mother's eyes.

With his hand buried in the top drawer of the dresser, he allowed himself to explore, stroking the smooth coolness of silk. He pulled out a green and light blue paisley scarf and pushed it deep into the pocket of his trousers. His heart racing, he meticulously refolded each of the items in the drawer before pushing the contents out of sight and closing the drawer against the face of the dresser. Mitchell polished away any evidence of his presence from the dresser and the door knobs with his handkerchief. If anyone from the group found out about his secret, his job would be in serious jeopardy. He couldn't afford to take risks. Also, this was not a good time to get distracted.

After he had erased all traces of his presence in Mrs. Owens home, Mitchell returned to the privacy of his car to call his contact with the name of the woman Mrs. Owens had been seen talking with the previous morning. He then received yet another assignment for the evening; a busy one at Dr. Pate's home, but nothing he couldn't pull off. He would finish up at the Pate residence, drive back to town, and then orient himself to Mrs. Stewart's neighborhood. On Sunday he would start familiarizing himself with her routine.

If Mrs. Owens had confided in this friend of hers, it could be problematic for the group. The group held a very narrow-minded opinion about having any attention directed toward their activities. It was obvious they would do anything to keep from being exposed. And, no one was irreplaceable. Another reason for Mitchell to toe the line.

Chapter Fourteen

Greg realized, too late, that he should have talked with Ramsey and Mary Beth alone, rather than involving the group. That had been his intention. But he had received a call on Friday afternoon confirming delivery and thanking him for a successful harvest. Like a fool, Greg had mentioned how he had allayed Mary Beth's "second thoughts." He had assured the caller everything was under control and told him he was going to Ramsey's for drinks Saturday evening. He hadn't counted on Mitchell getting word of the conversation and showing up at Ramsey's house.

The evening had started out like any other Saturday evening get together. Greg had arrived before Mary Beth. Ramsey, boy wonder of Blakely, offered him a beer. Asking, "Or has Leah refined all your pleasure receptors?"

"I'll have a beer," Greg had growled.

Before he had taken a drink, Mary Beth came in through the garage entrance. She walked across the den, directly to the kitchen and went behind the bar to greet Ramsey. As they embraced, Greg saw a guy enter the house through the same door Mary Beth had used.

"Well hello, you must be Dr. Pate. I'm Mitchell," he said, his brashness causing a commotion. Then, bowing grandly as he turned toward Mary Beth, he added, "And you must be the beautiful

Mary Beth." Mitchell turned toward Greg and shook his hand, introducing himself as he smiled broadly. He held up a bottle of wine and asked Ramsey for a corkscrew and glasses. Ramsey obliged him by opening a drawer for the corkscrew while Mary Beth, without comment, pulled four stemmed glasses from a cabinet.

Mitchell made a lavish production of pouring two drinks and handing them to Ramsey and Mary Beth. While Ramsey and Mary Beth stood by, their drinks in hand, he commenced pouring drinks for Greg and himself.

"First, a toast to our host and his lovely lady," he announced.

Raising his glass a second time, he beckoned the others to do the same and announced, "Be proud. You have cut your way through the constraints of bureaucracy creating an avenue of hope for people who, until now, had run out of hope." Everyone drank. Mary Beth stared suspiciously from Greg to Mitchell. After a moment, she lost interest in them and settled her gaze on Ramsey. She had wanted to tell him this Mitchell frightened her, but a warm feeling started to come over her and, for the first time in days, she began to relax.

Stunned by the entire display, Greg eyed Mitchell suspiciously. Ramsey's scowl extinguished any notion that he had enjoyed the intrusion of this uninvited guest.

He made his way around the bar to stand beside Greg and whispered curtly, "Where do you get off telling this jerk where I live and asking him into my home?"

Before Greg had time to explain that he had never laid eyes on the man and hadn't told him anything about Ramsey, Mitchell walked back to the door he had entered, when he followed Mary Beth inside, and announced, "I'd like you all to meet Vince. Vince was kind enough to drive me over in his van. Vince, meet Drs. Palmer and Pate. I think you know Mrs. Owens."

"Pleased to see you again," Vince nodded toward Mary Beth.

Mary Beth lifted a heavy hand toward Vince then excused herself to take a seat on the sofa.

As Vince turned, Greg and Ramsey caught sight of the right side of his face, and both men were more taken aback by Vince's disfigured appearance than anything else at that moment. Pleated at the corner of his eye, the ruddy skin stretched across his entire cheek, and the eye lid puckered slightly near the nose. As if he knew they were staring at him, Vince reeled around and left the room.

They focused their attention on Mary Beth who had sunk into the sofa, a blank stare on her face. Ramsey crossed the room, turning away from Mitchell as he passed, and sat beside her. Within minutes, he yawned and planted his head against the back of the sofa.

Mitchell studied his wristwatch for a long second, nodded to himself as if mentally recording the time, then broke into action. He opened the door to that led to the garage, and Vince came back inside accompanied by a slender young man whom Vince didn't bother to introduce. "Take care of these two. Get them comfy." Then he motioned toward Greg. "Wash this glass and put it back into the cabinet."

"Wait just a minute, Mitchell," Greg protested. "You can't just waltz in here like this and start ordering us around. What do you think you're doing? You owe me an explanation." Greg clenched his jaw as he stared at Mitchell. "*Where did this guy get off?*" Greg thought

"I owe you nothing," Mitchell responded harshly. "You wanted them to be convinced they had done the right thing. Well, now they're convinced." Then, speaking softly, so that Greg had to strain to hear him, he told him, "Dr. Palmer, I suggest you do exactly as you are told without wasting any more of my time."

Greg managed to clean the glass and place it in the cabinet without breaking it, despite his nervousness. He decided Mitchell had slipped something into the wine he served Ramsey and Mary Beth. In all probability the substance had been Rohypnol, a date rape drug. Greg wondered why Mitchell had done it and what he intended to do with them when they woke up.

Mitchell ordered Greg to help him lift Mary Beth. Sound asleep and heavy, like dead weight, she offered no resistance. They carried her through the garage to a van backed up in the driveway. The air wasn't as hot as it had been when Greg had arrived at Ramsey's house. A light wind made the evening almost pleasant. As the breeze caught her face, Mary Beth raised her head slightly. The stimulus wasn't enough to waken her. Mitchell stepped into the van first and offered his hand as Greg bore most of her weight and lifted her. The inside of the van contained two gurneys. They placed Mary Beth on one and pulled straps across her thighs and chest and fastened them. Once she was secure, Mitchell ordered Greg back inside the house. As he stepped down from the van, Greg tripped on a crack at the edge of the driveway separating the drive from the patio area. Mitchell yelled at him to pay attention. Vince sat on a fold down seat facing the rear of the van silently staring as the two men hauled Ramsey into the van. The slender, nameless man had disappeared.

After fastening Ramsey onto the second gurney, Mitchell escorted Greg to his car. His forearm carelessly resting on the window opening of the car, Mitchell belted out details of what Greg should say when questioned. Turning to leave, he spun a half circle, eyes dead on and reminded Greg, "And don't go looking for trouble. You're in deep enough already. I'll be in touch." Greg imagined Mitchell to be capable of making good on all of his threats.

Chapter Fifteen

Still trembling as he cut the engine, Greg laid his head against the cool chestnut steering wheel. Think. He had to think. Mitchell had told him to rehearse what he would need to say in case the authorities came to him for a statement. "I went to Ramsey's about six-thirty, I don't recall the exact time. It was a casual get together. Mary Beth was there; she usually is on weekends. After a while, it looked like they were tired of my company. They had been drinking, of course. Yes, I had some knowledge of Ramsey's penchant for Fentanyl, everyone at Blakely knew, didn't they? He told me he hadn't used in over two years. I wouldn't risk my patients with him to manage their anesthesia if I knew he was still shooting up. I left around eight. No, my wife can't confirm that; she's on South Padre Island with the kids."

Mitchell had rattled off the canned statement for Greg to repeat as easily as a waiter in a restaurant would list the chef's special of the day.

Greg had met Mitchell for the first time at Ramsey's. *How did Mitchell know where Ramsey lived and that he would be there? How did Mitchell know he had a wife and children? How would Mitchell have known they had gone to the beach with Leah's parents for the weekend?* It seemed Mitchell knew everything there was to know about Greg, yet Greg knew nothing of Mitchell. Greg realized he couldn't prove that Mitchell existed. He didn't know Mitchell's last name, his address, or his phone number.

He forced the door open and dragged himself from the car. He pushed the button and listened as the garage door creaked in protest at the order to go down. Inside the phone rang insistently. Greg stumbled around the island cabinet in the kitchen to answer. He didn't need anyone to know he had not been home. It was after nine already.

"Hello."

"Greg! It's me darling, did I wake you?" Leah said.

"No. No, baby. Well, I was dozing in front of the TV," he lied.

"I thought you sounded out of it," Leah laughed, flaring her hand over the granite countertop examining her perfectly manicured French tip nails. She tilted her left hand causing the kitchen light to dance on her diamond and platinum rings.

"I just this minute tucked the munchkins into their beds. They were worn out! You really should have come down with us. This fresh, salty air would clear the cobwebs. You work too much. Mother used to tell Daddy, 'Blakely Hospital won't close the doors if you aren't there for a few days.' The same goes for you. You're missing all the fun."

Leah chattered about the day at the beach. Greg contended she had never in her life worried about anything bigger than a broken nail or where to have the girls' birthday parties. How he wished he could share her ignorant bliss.

Faking a yawn, he said, "There's no place I'd rather be right now than with you, but I'm on call tomorrow. I'm happy knowing all my girls are having fun and that you'll be home soon. You can do me a favor and stop by the Bay Side Shrimp House before you leave the island and pick up a pound of those jumbo boiled shrimp for me, if you remember."

"For you, my darling I'll remember, I promise."

They said their goodnights. Greg's heart pounded as he hung up the phone.

His perfect plan had disintegrated into an absolutely horrific mess. The entire plot would have gone unnoticed if Mary Beth had kept the initial agreement. In fact Mitchell would have never shown up at Ramsey's had it not been for Mary Beth's sudden fit of moral consciousness. She had seemed like the ideal circulating nurse to help. She lived above her means, took call for the OR all the time for extra income, and, luckily, her fiancé just happened to be an anesthesiologist with a history of doping himself up with the Fentanyl he signed out for his patients.

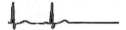

Ramsey always wore two sets of scrubs in the OR. He asserted this was a necessity because the surgeons insisted the thermostat be turned down in the operating rooms. Once, after having worked at Blakely about a month, Greg had witnessed Ramsey at the end of a case slipping a syringe into the chest pocket of the inside scrub top. Ramsey looked up to catch Greg watching him as he withdrew his hand. A few minutes later, Ramsey showed the circulator a syringe and squirted the liquid from it into the trash.

The circulator signed the narcotic sheet for the wasted narcotic. This confirmed the rumor Greg had heard in reference to Ramsey's history of drug abuse.

Ramsey didn't need the money he would gain from assisting with the organ harvest. The sole heir to a third generation ranching fortune, he didn't need to work at all. Yet Greg knew he couldn't afford to refuse. In theory, Greg figured the plot had been a win-win situation. Every detail had been covered. Even his idea to note on the code record an attempt at open heart massage had provided an explanation for the use of the chest tray to open the chest, if the case happened to be reviewed.

To Greg, it had seemed a stroke of fortune that so much money could be made without lying or cheating. He had made an ethical decision to save lives. Doctors encountered ethical dilemmas every day.

During medical school, he had read of the "Seattle God Committee," a group, formed in the Sixties, which was assigned the enormous task of deciding the fate of patients in kidney failure. The technology was new and dialysis machines were in short supply. The lucky ones would receive dialysis treatments. Those not fortunate enough to be selected were doomed to die of renal failure.

In the case of this harvest, the donor had nothing to lose. When Greg and the others had harvested the organs of this young man, who was brain-dead, they had actually helped to restore quality of life to several people. Everything had gone according to plan until Mary Beth developed that 'goody two-shoes' attitude and started complaining about it not being right.

The bedroom Greg shared with Leah stood silent and empty. Her laughter had left with her. They had been married since his second year of residency and had two small children. In a moment of weakness, he had responded to a call, a call too tempting to refuse. Greg had rehearsed, in his head, the perfectly laid plan as it had been presented to him. He had carried the plot further with his notion of ethically justifying the harvest. Now, he would be the only person traceable to this unimaginable criminal act. Mitchell's unwelcome visit had caused the perfect plan to rapidly spiral into an abysmal hell, with Greg in the middle of it. Greg knew for certain he would never see Ramsey or Mary Beth alive again.

Chapter Sixteen

The headlights bobbed as the van cantered along the rutted path toward the plane. At times the lights would reflect the fuselage of the Gulf Stream jet waiting for them. Vince sat in the passenger seat of the van. He focused his night vision binoculars on the plane. The ladder was down and the pilot and copilot stood at the tip of the left wing. Vince scanned the area and then gave the driver a 'thumbs up' indicating that he was clear to approach the plane. Had it not been safe, the van would have ambled off to the right, to avoid detection, and taken a detour down an old ranch road that led back into town.

Vince crawled into the back of the van. He had already drawn several vials of blood from both Ramsey Pate and Mrs. Owens and labeled them; these samples were packaged and taped to their right arms. He checked and recorded their vital signs and made certain the safety belts around their chests and legs were secure.

Even though the effects of the drug Mitchell had slipped into their drinks would probably last for several hours, Vince administered an additional sedative to each of them intravenously.

The van backed up to the plane. Vince opened the van door from the inside. The pilot and copilot nodded, and Vince released the locks that secured the gurneys in the van. The four men worked to pull the gurneys, one at a time, out of the van. After collapsing the wheeled frames of the gurneys, they carried them up the ladder and into the plane. Within minutes they had the two secure within the cabin of the plane and the gurneys back inside the van.

As the plane climbed into the night sky and vanished into the blackness among the stars, Vince opened the envelope the pilot had handed him earlier. His payment was more than he had made in a year as a medic.

Vince climbed into the passenger seat of the van. He handed Dillon his share of the money. Dillon put the money in his shirt pocket as he shifted the van into gear.

"Thanks man," Dillon said and nodded toward Vince, a crooked smile brightening his face.

After they left the Pate house for the second time that night, Dillon stopped at the first self-service car wash he found. He carefully vacuumed the cargo area before he hosed the thick layer of dust off the outside of the van.

Vince had adjusted to this ritual. Dillon always drove the last leg of a job, stopping off at a car wash to clean the van before driving to his rundown apartment building. He would back into the parking space closest to the main entrance of the complex, kill the engine, hand the keys to Vince and say, "See ya, man." Vince developed his own habit of watching Dillon go into his apartment. Dillon would take his shoes off at the door, switch the light on, count to five then turn it off. When the light went off, his "all clear" sign had been given to Vince.

Once, when they had been waiting for a plane to arrive, Vince had told Dillon about a fishing trip he had taken to Canada. He described the secluded cabin near a stream filled with trout. "Someday I'm going to buy myself a place just like that and when I leave Texas, I'll never look back," he had said. "You'd love it up there. Tall spruce trees that touch the sky. The air is cool and clear, none of this stifling heat."

Dillon had stared down at his hands. "How will you find a place like that from way down here in the middle of Texas?"

Vince described the ads he had seen in the back of back-to-nature type magazines. "There's one in British Columbia not far from Vancouver, a place called Duncan Ridge. I'll show up with the money and one of my IDs. When I offer them full price, they won't be able to refuse. Dillon, money levels the playing field. Remember that."

Chapter Seventeen

Situated on ten acres about fifteen minutes from town, Ramsey Pate's palatial home sat secluded among Live Oaks. The land had been carved out of the backside of his father's ranch. Ramsey and his first wife Margaret had had the house built.

Just days prior to their wedding, Ramsey's dad had presented them a check with enough zeroes to build a very nice home. "So I can be close to my grandchildren," he announced. Only three years had passed before a new girlfriend distracted Ramsey away from Margaret, and from any plans of starting a family.

Ramsey's lawyer had offered her a generous cash settlement in exchange for a divorce and Margaret's signature relinquishing any claim on the property. Complementing the offer, a letter from the lawyer informed her that the house was actually a part of the Pate family ranch. Title to the land had never been transferred. Ramsey owned the house. His father owned the land. Margaret no longer had a home or a husband.

Most mornings waking up to the thought of Ramsey and his philandering had made Margaret so nauseated she didn't care where she lived or whether she lived. Without Ramsey, the house didn't matter. She had accepted the cash and bought a small place in New Mexico with an old adobe house and a small, neglected apple orchard. Margaret had packed the Land Rover and had taken her broken heart to Cloudcroft vowing never to set foot on the Pate Ranch again.

Ramsey's nearest neighbors, an elderly couple who lived about a half mile down the road, had arrived home about midnight from their granddaughter's wedding and reception. Mr. Clemman had dozed off to sleep when he was awakened by the insistent barking of his dog. When he looked out, the sky directly over the Pate home glowed white, like noontime. Mr. Clemman called Ramsey. No answer. He called the volunteer fire department.

By the time the fire trucks arrived, raging red flames leapt toward the sky. Huge gray and black clouds rose to hide any stars. "If anyone was in there, they're goners now," said a burly off-duty patrolman, his white western shirt marked with soot.

The bright lights from the dying flames and flashing lights from sheriffs' cars, an ambulance, and several fire trucks were visible from three miles away. Ramsey's dad stood in his side yard, his eyes fixed on the sight as the sheriff spoke. "Mr. Pate, do you know if Ramsey might have been at home?"

Mr. Pate, standing erect, his razor-thin shoulders trembling, could only shake his head. His short, white hair reflected light as he moved. Ramsey was his only son, his only child. Mr. Pate felt a grievous void in his chest. His heart told him Ramsey wasn't home. However, he didn't want to believe Ramsey was dead.

Chapter Eighteen

Sunday after church Aubrey stood, in the deeply arched entry of the sanctuary, waiting for Eric. She caught sight of Douglas standing beside her car. Aubrey noticed how the fine lines at the edges of his eyes failed to disappear when his smile faded. The bright, midday light danced on the silver hair lacing his temples. He had gained a little weight over the years, and had grown stockier, as his Scot-Irish mother had mentioned the last time they had visited her in central Texas. Aubrey tried to retrieve the details of their last visit; it had been at least two years. She remembered they had stopped off at Trish and Jim's on the way home. Aubrey first met Douglas at Trish and Jim's engagement party.

Aubrey had been a freshman in college. A friend of hers was going to be married and the girl's dad threw a huge engagement party at the family ranch to introduce his future son-in-law, Jim, to everyone. Trisha had asked Aubrey if she would come as the date of Jim's old college friend. Douglas had graduated and commenced his climb up the corporate ladder in the oil leasing business.

"He's more preppy than cowboy, but Jim said, on campus he was a hunk," Trisha had said.

Douglas had been one of the few guys at the barbeque who did not have on a pair of starched Wranglers with a faded circle on the hip pocket, the mark made by a tobacco tin, an embossed leather belt with a silver buckle the size of a postcard, and a snap up western style shirt. Instead of jeans and western shirt, he had worn khakis with a Ranger-style belt and an oxford shirt. His concession to cowboy style had been his brown roper boots. Not a cowboy, but definitely a hunk.

As the stars started to light up the blue black sky, Douglas asked her to dance. That long ago night, when he had held her close, Aubrey knew she would marry this man.

"*What happened to those wonderful years?*" she thought as she looked at the one to whom she had so freely given her heart.

Douglas waved to her. She joined him at the passenger side of her car.

"Where's Eric?" he asked.

"Putting his things away, he served as acolyte today. Did one of the guys cancel?" Douglas and three of his friends had a standing Tee time at the local country club on Sunday at eleven. Occasionally, if one of the guys in his foursome cancelled, Douglas asked Eric to join them.

He brushed his brows back and forth with his fingers. "Aubrey, you'd better sit down. I have some bad news."

Douglas hesitated. Begging the air to formulate the words, he blurted, "I need to tell you, Ramsey Pate's house burned last night. He and Mary Beth are dead."

"That's impossible," she stared at him in disbelief.

Douglas repeated the last sentence, looking directly into her eyes.

Aubrey covered her face with both hands, separating herself from this harsh reality. Douglas pulled a folded white handkerchief from his hip pocket and handed it to her, then gently rested his hand on her shoulder.

"How did it happen?" a stunned Aubrey asked.

"No one knows yet, at least there's no report of a cause. According to the TV news, it was like an inferno. Burned to the ground. Anyone inside had no chance of survival. Mary Beth's car was in the drive, and what was left of Ramsey's vehicles were still in the garage."

She laced her fingers together and pressed her hands to her forehead, tenting her eyes as she looked up to Douglas. Peering into Douglas's eyes, she groped for a way to comprehend all this, to make some sense of what he had said. "Are they sure Ramsey and Mary Beth were there? Maybe they went out with someone, in their car. Maybe they took a walk. She told me they were going to the club for dinner. They could have gone somewhere else afterward. We had a date for brunch."

Douglas wearily shook his head as he kept his eyes fixed on the entrance of the church wishing for the heavy, dark stained door to open and Eric to bound through it and save him from this moment. The agony of Aubrey's empty gaze reminded him of the evening he had told her he intended to move out of the house.

Aubrey sat on the edge of the passenger seat with her legs crossed, dark pink toe nails peeked out of the open-toe pale pink pumps, one foot kicked air and the other sat firmly planted on the pavement. Her mind replayed the conversation she had with Mary Beth the day before. Cassie was to have spent the night with a friend. Was she wakened this morning to the news of her mother's death?

Sidetracking the concern at hand, Aubrey wondered which of her siblings would be there for Eric if something happened to Douglas and her. Certainly not her sister Anna! Her involvement with family consisted of a preprinted Christmas card each year. Anna had no desire to maintain a relationship with her siblings. Her life revolved around her religion and her husband. Living a thousand miles away insured she remain protected from any semblance of family contact. When Aubrey and Douglas had planned a trip east to take Eric for a visit, Anna had announced it would be inconvenient.

Jack, her brother, lived a thousand miles north of Texas. Although he didn't visit often, he phoned at least once a month. He recently developed the habit of sending pictures of himself on fishing trips. Eric's last birthday present had been a Cabela fly-fishing rod and reel with a note promising a fishing trip on the Clark Fork River for trout when school ended for the summer. Even though he had no experience with children, Aubrey felt certain he would be the one to take care of Eric.

Douglas motioned toward the church as he saw their son crossing the street. "There's Eric. Come on let's get you to the house."

"What about your car?"

"Kim can come back with me to pick it up, then follow me to the house in my car."

At the house, Douglas hung around for awhile and made some tea. He insisted on taking Eric home with him, so Aubrey could rest. But once they left, there was no way for Aubrey to rest. If she closed her eyes to sleep, an image of Mary Beth, reaching out to her with cupped hands, forced its way through the darkness.

Catching sight of her fly rod in the corner, she thought, "*Why not?*" The instructor had touted the sport as an opportunity to escape stressors.

With the ferrules connected, she held the grip of the rod against her cheek and eyeballed the alignment of the guides; satisfied, she then held the reel in position while she tightened the seat lock. She worked the line through the guides. A bright orange swatch of yarn, which she tied onto the tippet, stood in for a fly.

Standing in an open area of the backyard, Aubrey planted her thumb on top as she gripped the cork handle. Her right hand brought the rod straight up then she slung it forward. During the back and forth stroke, she recited the phrase, "Candy Cane," giving enough pause for the line to make an arc. She willed the orange practice fly to land on a flower pot by the back fence, as she focused her eyes on the rim of the pot and directed the tip of the rod toward it. With each cast she repeated this process, targeting different objects.

The act of concentrating on every detail of her movements helped to improve her casting technique; it did little to push the sad news of the tragic fire from her mind. Convinced the case in OR Ten was directly related to the fire, Aubrey thought, "*It couldn't have been an accident; accidents are never that convenient.*"

"*Had they been murdered?*" Aubrey dared not utter the words out loud.

Somber, solemn minutes turned into hours as Aubrey watched the purple shade settle over the deep pink western sky.

When she had crawled into bed, Aubrey opened the novel she had started the previous night and tried to read. She couldn't stay focused on the book, so she replaced the string of fishing line she used as a bookmark and laid the book on the nightstand. Opening the top drawer of the nightstand and searching for a tissue to blot her eyes, her fingers retracted after touching the cold steel clip filled with bullets for Douglas's gun. He had bought the nine millimeter hand gun over much protest from Aubrey. There had been reports of robberies in the area and he insisted on having the gun for protection.

Aubrey had conceded to Douglas's demands and had allowed him to keep the gun in the house, provided the gun and the ammunition were separated. The gun was kept hidden on the shelf near the bedroom window and the clip hidden in the night stand drawer. She would remind Douglas to take the gun with him, since she had no intention of ever firing the thing.

Chapter Nineteen

A pale, summer sun peeked through the window. Aubrey rubbed her swollen eyes, trying to clear the fog of a restless night. The aching in her chest confirmed the reality of what had seemed like a nightmare. The vision of Mary Beth holding her own heart had interrupted her thoughts so many times Aubrey had begun to accept its virtuality.

At work, a mournful quiet shrouded the unit, replacing the usual exuberant Monday morning conversation about the weekend. The staff gathered in the break room, solemnly sharing bits of information they had heard about the tragedy. One of the nurse's exclaimed, "Our friendly ghost is at it again; my lab coat, fresh from the cleaners, is on the hook." The nurse had turned the unit upside down in search of it. Inside the pocket, the nurse found a pink sticky note attached to a candy bar. "Look, she even replaced my candy." This injection of gaiety lightened their spirits a bit

Any unexplained occurrence or unconfessed prank was attributed to the unit's ghost, and the ghost always left a pink sticky

note with a broadened u that was drawn on with a fluorescent marker to form a smile.

Aubrey isolated herself and focused on her paperwork. She printed a revised schedule for the day then busied herself with the PACU charges. Each patient was listed in the log book along with procedure, surgeon, anesthesiologist, nurse, the admission time, dismissal time, care unit dismissed to, and any particulars about their post anesthesia stay. Even though the same data was entered in the computer, the department maintained a parallel hard copy of the log; and the plan was to continue this course until the entire patient charting system was computerized.

The log book was used mainly as a tool for quality improvement and patient tracking. Most of the information Aubrey needed for data collection could be written in the comment section, an old habit from the year she spent working in the ICU.

PACU charges were based on half-hour increments of time, after a minimum time of one hour for each patient that came from the OR. Each week a computer-generated printout was checked against the log for accuracy. Aubrey was responsible for clarifying any discrepancies on this report. If a patient was admitted directly to the ICU, as was the case with some procedures, the charges had to be credited. Usually this paperwork was dreaded as a boring task. Today, Aubrey welcomed the monotony.

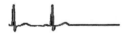

Valerie and Cindy served as the planners and organizers of the unit. They were already on the phone arranging for food to be sent to Ramsey and Mary Beth's families. Cindy had posted a list of volunteers from ICU listing those staff members willing to cover the schedule over the next few days. The OR Director had called a meeting for all staff and delayed the start time for the OR. That meant the recovery unit would not have any patients for at least two hours.

Valerie leaned into Aubrey's office, "Rebecca asked for you to come to her office."

"I need to go to the ICU to check these charges. Can it wait?"

"She sounded serious."

"Okay, thanks," Aubrey said, thinking Rebecca had read her message.

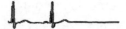

Rebecca Krantz, the OR director, had been employed at the hospital since the summer after high school. Her first job had been in Central Supply cleaning and sterilizing instruments. Then she worked summers as a scrub tech in the OR until she graduated from college. After passing her licensing examinations, she worked as a Registered Nurse circulating cases in the Operating Rooms.

When the past director retired, Rebecca was the only qualified candidate considered to take the position. Rebecca knew all there was to know about the people, the politics, and the patients at Blakely. Nothing escaped her scrutiny.

Aubrey walked into the reception area of the OR office. From there she could see a man seated facing Rebecca. Rebecca motioned for Aubrey to come inside and sit in the remaining chair. "Come on in and close the door please," Rebecca addressed

Aubrey. She then made formal introductions, "Aubrey Stewart, this is Detective Jon Stokes. Detective Stokes, Aubrey Stewart."

Aubrey took his extended hand as she wondered how this young man could possibly be qualified to investigate the death of her friends. He didn't look old enough to be out of college. From the looks of the smooth skin on his face, with the exception of one, angry, whitehead on his chin, Aubrey doubted the detective was old enough to shave.

"Aubrey, Detective Stokes is here to ask some questions about Mary Beth and Ramsey. He wanted to talk to you first, since you apparently were the last one to talk with Mary Beth before," Rebecca paused, as if forcing her mouth to utter the appropriate words, "Before Saturday night." Rebecca then said, "Excuse me," and left them alone.

Aubrey fought to remain composed, a futile effort. Everything became blurry as tears welled in her eyes. She bit her lower lip and attempted to speak without crying. "I didn't see her. I only spoke to her on the phone." Truth be known, the tears were in sympathy for Mary Beth and Ramsey but also for the anger she harbored toward Mary Beth for deceiving her.

"Mrs. Stewart, I would like to offer my condolences. I also want you to know that I intend do everything possible to understand how this tragedy happened."

The young detective paused, allowing Aubrey some time.

"Do they know for a fact Mary Beth and Ramsey were there when it happened?" Aubrey wondered how much of an investigation they were conducting.

"Based on all the evidence so far, it's reasonably certain your friend, Mrs. Owens, and her fiancé, Dr. Pate, were in the house when the fire started."

"Do they know what caused the fire?" Aubrey asked.

"I don't believe that has been determined yet, ma'am. The fire marshal is investigating it. He has mentioned the gas hot water heater as a possible source. In the same press release, he said that it was only speculation at this point."

Detective Stokes, resuming control of the questions, leaned closer to Aubrey and looked straight at her with doleful, brown eyes. "Mrs. Stewart, it appears your friend was a victim of a terrible accident. My job is to discover what did happen. You can help. Can you tell me about the last time you spoke with Mrs. Owens, if you remember?"

"How well I remember! It was Saturday. We played phone tag all day; when we did connect, we made a date for brunch on Sunday."

"When did you last see her?"

"On Friday morning, she was talking to Dr. Palmer and she seemed distracted and melancholic. We walked in together."

"You said she seemed distracted on Friday morning. Tell me about that."

"I was on my way into the hospital. Mary Beth and Dr. Palmer were standing by his car; they seemed to be engrossed in conversation. She just looked worried, that's all." Aubrey hesitated to share what she thought might have contributed to Mary Beth's worries.

She continued, struggling to choose the correct words. "She told me she was going to Ramsey's for drinks Saturday night, then to dinner at the country club. I figured she would spend the night, she usually did. They were engaged."

"Did she say anything more about her plans?"

"The time, she planned to be at his house at six-thirty. She was specific about that. Also, she intended to make an omelet for me on Sunday."

Detective Stokes could see Aubrey had wearied from her recollections of the previous week. "I want you to take my card," he said, dislodging a stiff business card from a new leather folder that held a shiny, untarnished badge. "Please call me if you think of anything else." He stood and asked Aubrey if she could direct him to Mary Beth's locker. Rebecca had given him the locker number and permission to inspect the contents. Aubrey led him into the hall and in the direction of the Women's Lounge.

"Rebecca has the master key; she should be in there. If she isn't, then ask Margie," Aubrey pointed to a dark haired young woman in scrubs walking toward the lounge. "Just tell her you're looking for Mrs. Krantz. She'll escort you back."

Chapter Twenty

Vince sat on the bench facing the gray granite headstone. *April 22, 1996,* freshly engraved underneath his mother's name and date of birth, contrasted with the other lettering. *COLSTEN*, spread across the top, then down and to the left *Vincent Ralph, September 7, 1945 –December 8, 1967*, and *Genny Grace, October 12, 1947* on the right, had all darkened to the color of coal. Vince arranged a bouquet of pale yellow roses in the attached vase between his parents' names, then poured water to the brim.

A small rabbit crouched against the ground, frozen in place, one brown eye trained on Vince. Vince didn't move, and, after a few minutes the rabbit began to chomp on a clover stem, and then gobble the entire white blossom. Soon a second rabbit, a bit more cautious of Vince's presence, joined his bigger friend under the tree. The two continued to enjoy their breakfast, moist with water from the sprinkler, as Vince watched, memorizing the scene: the headstone; the faded flag posted by his father's name; and the bronze plaque at the foot of his grave; the slight hollow, of the earth, in front of his mother's name; the Colsten family obelisk, keeping watch over a dozen souls; the sunlight, filtered by the Live Oak; the quiet; these two young rabbits; and himself, slouched here on this concrete bench, alone.

Vince rubbed along his right temple to relieve the twitching that sometimes turned into a spasm. His head pounded with the pain of guilt. Knowing that you're delivering organs that have been taken from a person that was already brain-dead didn't concern Vince so much, but he'd taken a wrong turn and had gone too far. His mother's voice rang in his ear, "You can sink so low that you lose your way, your sense of values." Those were the exact words she had spoken a few years earlier, when Vince came home bitter and full of hate.

She had also tried to tell him that he was the same as before he got wounded. "What's inside, your very core, that's the real you. You can't let a scar change you, Son." but the world didn't see him that way.

Vince had used up all his savings to complete his premed degree, all for nothing. All the medical schools he had applied to had turned him down. He had kept all his rejections letters, tucked away at home in the shoe box that previously held all his high school football memorabilia.

When he had dumped the old stuff out and had tossed it into the trash can, his mother had begged him to keep it. Vince wasn't that person anymore and he didn't want to be reminded of how he had looked before the right side of his face had been shattered. He replaced pictures of the handsome young man in the black and gold football uniform with pictures of a wounded soldier, before and after several stages of reconstructive surgery. Tiny plates and screws held his cheek bone in place. The scars had been revised, and the revisions had been revised. A new eyelid had been fashioned from his foreskin. Vince remembered wondering what the doctor would have used if he had already been circumcised. The last picture on the stack showed him after the prosthetic eye had been inserted into the socket.

For as long as he could remember, he had wanted to be a doctor, but he had never been accepted into medical school. And he hadn't been able to land a decent job, until he received the application from the Group. Transporting a kidney for a fringe operation was one thing; but the last couple of assignments had involved too much.

Now, he regretted having gone to work for the scum. Vince also felt responsible for Dillon's involvement. Dillon didn't have anyone in his corner, never did have.

In one of the few conversations he initiated about himself, Dillon had told Vince something of his childhood and how the teacher had made him sit by himself in the cafeteria and eat alone. Socially, Dillon remained in the third grade, sitting by himself, watching.

The rabbits frolicked in front of Vince, no longer skittish of his presence. The sound of an approaching car caused them to disappear deep beneath the heavy cover of a Juniper standing at the corner of the grave plot. Vince continued his vigil, sitting on the bench, wishing he could talk with his mom, until the noonday sun forced him to take cover.

Chapter Twenty-One

After lunch, Aubrey took the time to finish her reports. The finalized charges had to be entered by four o'clock for the billing department's access. Two patients had been charged erroneously. Both patients had gone directly back to the ICU postoperatively and should not have been billed any time in the PACU. One patient had a procedure which required ICU care post operatively. The second patient had been in the ICU on the ventilator; Dr. Palmer's case on Thursday night, Aubrey figured.

The tracheotomy patient's name didn't match the name on the daily census for Monday. Aubrey approached Regina, the unit secretary in the ICU, about the discrepancy.

"That patient was admitted Saturday night," Regina said referring to the name on the census for Monday.

"What about this one?" Aubrey asked showing her the name of the trach patient.

"Oh, that kid. I think he died," Regina said. "His chart is over there," she added, pointing to a counter covered with a mountain of manila folders.

Aubrey found the chart and opened it, glancing through the progress records for an operative report to make certain he had gone directly back to the ICU after the trach. The patient was an eighteen-year-old who had been comatose since a motor vehicle accident. His

EEGs were flat, and the progress records indicated the doctors had discussed the grave prognosis with the family. Dr. Palmer had entered notes concerning the need for a tracheotomy tube. Aubrey continued to read the progress notes. The family had refused organ donation and had requested the body be cremated. This last note had been signed by Dr. Palmer, not the primary physician for the patient.

The form releasing the body of the patient to the crematory also carried Dr. Palmer's signature. Aubrey wondered why he had not deferred this 'busy work'. He never hung around long enough after a procedure to look for a family member to tell them what he had done, let alone offer to do something so menial. The notion of Dr. Palmer waiting for the release of a body to the funeral home, especially in the middle of the night, seemed too unlikely to imagine.

"That means he had to have been in OR Ten when I left the hospital," Aubrey thought.

After she had returned the chart to the heap destined for the Medical Records Department and headed back toward the PACU, Aubrey's head reeled with the revelation that she had witnessed the stealthy harvest of this young man's organs even though his parents had signed a refusal form. That would explain Mary Beth's strange behavior and the encounter at the loading dock.

Rebecca sat at her desk, engrossed in the paperwork before her. "Rebecca, I need to speak with you, if you have a minute," Aubrey said. Rebecca nodded and motioned for Aubrey to sit down. Aubrey pulled her chair closer to the desk before she sat down. "To resolve all the discrepancies for the unit charges, I had to credit a couple of patients from ICU. Were you aware of a trach on Thursday night?"

"Not until after the fact," she spoke without looking directly at Aubrey. "I let Dr. Palmer know, in no uncertain terms, he would likely be called in when the code team meets. He explained that the patient wasn't expected to live anyway. That was why he had postponed taking him to the OR earlier in the day to be trached." Rebecca went on to tell Aubrey how she wished Dr. Palmer would have taken the case to the OR after his last scheduled surgery that day. "Or, for that matter, do it in the unit, if it's that late at night. He said the patient's heart just bradyed down and went flat line. The outcome likely would have been the same if it had been a scheduled case in the middle of the day. I have all these red flags popping up in my mind. Was Ramsey on top of everything? Did he miss subtle clues with the patient's heart rate that could have turned things around? Given his history, that was my first concern," she said with a knowing look toward Aubrey.

Rebecca continued. "Friday I reviewed the anesthesia preop. All his labs were within normal range. Three consecutive EEGs showed nothing but reflexive activity. The parents were going to be forced to make a decision soon. Considering he had the endotracheal tube for over a week, the trach was indicated. Maybe it was providential that it happened the way it did," Rebecca shrugged, her thin brows arching over almond shaped brown eyes.

"A sentinel event is not exactly what I would like to think of as providential, or what I would want to leave unaddressed through the weekend, but the budget committee meeting occupied most of my day. Greg happened to be the only person assigned to the case that I spoke with on Friday. Unfortunately, I never had an opportunity to ask Ramsey or Mary Beth for their feedback." Her eyes shifted toward the window. She had been close friends with Mary Beth, as well as Ramsey.

"They popped in here the other afternoon, Mary Beth and Ramsey, happy as larks, on their way to a meet with their wedding planner," Rebecca's spoke as she turned to face Aubrey. Her voice softened as she continued. "Lance had designed wedding bands for us," she stretched the fingers of her left hand, perfectly manicured with coral colored nail polish, out across the top of her desk and gently brushed the back of her ring finger with the middle three fingers of her right hand, "we had taken the sketch to Mike Swanson. Then Lance had that stroke." Tears clouded Rebecca's eyes.

With her head toward her lap, Aubrey aligned the tips of her fingers and pressed her palms together. It had been well over a year since Rebecca's boyfriend, Dr. Lance Murphy, had suffered a stroke that paralyzed one side of his body and left him unable to speak. Rebecca had never been so candid about her loss. She was the solid rock of the department, never one to over-share. Aubrey braced her chin on her thumbs, daring to look at Rebecca. The director of the department sat with pen in hand, back in charge, her attention on the document before her.

Aubrey considered excusing herself and leaving Rebecca to her own work, but she needed answers. "Do you know if Dr. Palmer knew the family?" She asked. Since Dr Palmer had documented in the progress notes that he had signed the body over to the crematory, Aubrey could inquire about this without any suggestion of impropriety.

"No. Not that I'm aware. Why do you ask?"

Aubrey told Rebecca some of what she had discovered from the chart. "It seems really odd to me that Dr. Palmer would go to such lengths. It's so unlike him to do anything he can delegate. You know how he is, Rebecca. Why would he do all that in the middle of the night?"

Clearing her throat, Rebecca responded to Aubrey. "This department has its share of personality types; believe me, I know. Logically though, we can't find fault with Greg for being attentive." Rebecca restacked the papers and added, "You've had a long day. Go home and get some rest. We're down to three ORs and there are enough nurses in the recovery room to cover the cases."

Aubrey left for the day, but she couldn't get Mary Beth out of her mind. Driving home, she tried to imagine plausible scenarios to explain their deaths. Nothing fit. Thursday night's events, especially the sight of Mary Beth in the OR, kept invading her thoughts. A patient dies in the operating room and, of the three people in the OR during the procedure, two of them supposedly burn to death in a house fire. Somehow there had to be a connection. Mary Beth's melancholy on Friday, when she had been talking with Dr. Palmer, forced Aubrey to believe if the fire was not an accident, Dr. Palmer had to have been involved.

Chapter Twenty-Two

Malcolm waddled across the alley toward Aubrey as she opened the driver's door of her car. Holding onto his bright red leash, Mrs. Leland waved to her. "Are you all right dear? I didn't see you at all yesterday. You weren't sick, were you?"

Aubrey bent to pet Malcolm, his tail moving back and forth like a windshield wiper set on high speed. "No, I wasn't sick." She stood, her eyes making contact with Mrs. Leland's squinted gaze. Despite her broad-brimmed straw hat, Mrs. Leland still had a problem with the glare of the afternoon sun. Aubrey invited her into the house. Mrs. Leland released Malcolm's leash and allowed him to go into the house ahead of her to investigate the kitchen floor. Aubrey told her about the fire and the likelihood that Ramsey and Mary Beth were dead.

Mrs. Leland covered her open mouth with her hand and gasped, "I had no idea. I saw that on the news. Oh my, you poor thing. It never crossed my mind that they were your friends. I should have known. After all, you've been at Blakely forever. You know everyone there. And they actually burned to death right there in the house, is that what they're saying at the hospital? Wait until I tell Jesse; she'll never believe what you have been through. And to think, I sat right over there and didn't even know," she shook her head in disbelief. "You have to call me if I can do anything at all for you. I can watch after Eric. He can stay with me or I can come over here, whatever you want."

Pausing long enough to inhale and sweep a loose strand of silver hair from her face, Mrs. Leland continued, "Now, was she that fleshy brunette with the sickly, yellow complexion. That nurse friend of yours I met right after Cal and I moved here?"

"No, that's Lisa," Aubrey said. "She has lost a lot of weight since you saw her." True enough, Lisa's skin did have a somewhat sallow color in the winter. Aubrey would have never called it sickly. She silently chuckled as she thought about the way her neighbor pictured her friends and wondered what terms Mrs. Leland might use to describe her.

"Mary Beth had auburn hair and big brown eyes. She was shorter than me," Aubrey held her hand at her chin and said, "About five foot five, five six; very pretty." She paused, watching the elderly lady absorb this information.

"Of course, now I remember." Mrs. Leland spoke, her eyes wide with surprise. "She used to come over here often with her little girl. Christmas, that was the last time I saw her." She nodded and looked at Aubrey for confirmation.

"Yes, that's her daughter Cassie. She and Eric ate almost all the homemade fudge you brought over."

"It's a thousand wonders they didn't get sick." The momentary delight in her face at the memory withered as she continued, "How sad for that poor child. Losing her mother like that. Where is the little dear now?"

"In town, with her grandparents. Mary Beth's sister, Sarah, has come in from Dallas. She's helping to look after her."

Once she had obtained enough information to impress her friend, Mrs. Jesse Willard, Mrs. Leland took Malcolm's leash and commenced saying her goodbyes. She turned back toward Aubrey, apologizing as she spoke.

"I'm sorry to have to ask, what with all you have on your mind and all, but my black iris, the "Snake's Head" it should be in bloom in a few days and I was hoping you would bring your camera over and photograph it for me. If it's a bother, just say so and I'll try to find someone else."

Aubrey assured her it would not be any bother as she showed her friend out.

The telephone demanded her attention the instant Aubrey closed the door. Hurrying over to it, she snatched up the receiver. "Hello," she said.

"Aubrey," Douglas spoke, "I called you at work, but they said you had left for the day. I could pick up something for dinner and come over; that is, if you don't mind."

"I don't mind at all, in fact I'll welcome it. Eric should be home from school anytime. Bring Kimberly if you like." Aubrey didn't have the desire to be caustic.

"Thanks, I'll ask her. See you in a few minutes."

Aubrey watched the televised news clip of the charred, gray rubble that had been Ramsey's house. The chimney rose above the dusty gray mound as the lone marker of existence. Locked inside those ashes were the secrets of Mary Beth and Ramsey's last thoughts. A strand of bright yellow plastic tape sealed the ruins.

Aubrey brewed tea and busied herself unloading the dishwasher. It hadn't been so long ago that she and Mary Beth had sat here, in the kitchen, sharing their innermost secrets.

It had been when Douglas had moved out. Mary Beth didn't have a date that weekend and had not scheduled herself to take call for the OR. This had been unusual, since she typically volunteered for extra call to support herself and Cassie. She had spent the entire day with Aubrey trying to convince her that she would go on living, even if Douglas never returned. Soon after that, Mary Beth and Ramsey were engaged. All of Mary Beth's free time lately had been spent with Ramsey.

When Douglas walked into the kitchen, Aubrey clicked the TV off and turned away to wipe her eyes. Douglas cleared his throat and busied himself putting ice in a glass for his tea and then poured a cup of hot tea for Aubrey. He sat down at the bar with her.

Aubrey detailed for him the events leading up to the deaths of Dr. Pate and Mary Beth. "Add the fact that Dr. Palmer came forward and volunteered a statement because he had been at Ramsey's house for drinks. That's a classic case of the guilty party trying to appear innocent."

"Aubrey, aren't you getting a little carried away? Suppose he did harvest the guy's organs without authorization, it's absurd to think he would kill everyone involved in the case."

"No, I'm not getting carried away. I'm trying my best to figure it all out. Nothing else adds up. All these crazy, little isolated bits are connected, somehow. It's just too odd. The image of Mary Beth at the loading dock bothers me; then, her with Dr Palmer in the parking lot. I know her. I've known her for years. She was anxious, even fearful about something. I refuse to believe she and Ramsey Pate died in an accidental fire. Neither of them smoked. If a candle did happen to tump over, two able-bodied adults should be capable of containing any fire. The hot water heater thing seems like a long shot. Besides, you always think I get carried away."

"That's because you often do. Aubrey, you should just allow the police to do their job. Let them handle it." Douglas poured himself another glass of tea.

"Like they do other deaths? Remember when Dr. Crawford overdosed and died in the OR? Rumors flew like blackbirds. She had been the victim of a love triangle, she had refused to go along with some scam, she had been a drug user in medical school, and, the biggie, that she had never been properly licensed as an MD. The feeble effort they called an investigation produced more questions than answers, at least for the most of us who thought we had known her."

"Initially, there were lots of rumors. Because Rebecca Krantz used hospital bureaucracy to delay the investigation. Once the hospital administrator allowed the police department to do their work, they ruled it a suicide. Heck Aubrey, the syringe beside her had her fingerprints on it. What was it they said, instead of dosing herself up on whatever she was addicted to, she accidentally took the wrong thing?"

Aubrey couldn't believe it. Douglas remembered the most negative theory about Dr. Crawford's death. "No one ever proved she had a problem with drug addiction. They found Sufenta out of place. It had been stacked in the narcotic box compartment where Fentanyl would usually be kept. Since it's about five times more potent than Fentanyl, it could very well cause an overdose. That doesn't mean she did it."

"Like now. For convenience sake, they'll call it an accidental fire. Never mind the early death of a patient. Doesn't it bother you that someone could be up to no good?"

"Look, you want someone to blame, that's natural; you're friend is dead. Dwelling on it won't change a thing. This isn't a movie, Aubrey. It's real life." Douglas appealed to her sense of reason.

Aubrey despised his logic. She was wasting her breath trying to get him to understand. Later, lying in bed, staring up at the dark shadows waltzing across the ceiling, she decided she would tell Detective Stokes about her suspicions. He seemed to be the young industrious sort, perhaps he would take her seriously.

Chapter Twenty-Three

Greg's pulse throbbed in his ears. A drink would calm him, but he needed to stay sharp. That cowboy detective was an aggravation, requesting to speak with him again! He had given a statement and had answered all the detective's questions earlier in the day and managed to stay calm through the process. Wade had said he wanted to clear up a couple of details, whatever that meant.

"Dr. Palmer, you remember my partner, Detective Stokes. He had a couple of items he wanted to get straight in his head before we laid this thing to rest. I hope you don't mind."

"Of course," Greg Palmer said, nonchalantly obliging him.

Detective Stokes glanced toward Detective Wade as if waiting for his cue before addressing Dr. Palmer. "Sir," he said after Detective Wade gave him a slight nod, "I was wondering if you could tell us about a conversation you had with Mrs. Owens on Friday morning. I believe you met her in the hospital parking lot."

"I didn't meet her there. I drove into the parking lot as Mary Beth, that is, Mrs. Owens, walked past. We had a 'good morning' type chat. That was it. Why do you ask?"

Detective Stokes ignored the question and continued. "Did Mrs. Owens express she might have had a concern, something that was bothering her?"

"No. She did not. I just told you it was a greeting, nothing more."

"Mrs. Aubrey Stewart, a friend of Mrs. Owens, said she saw you and Mrs. Owens talking and Mrs. Owens appeared to be troubled about something."

Greg Palmer felt the rush of color flood his face. His pulse quickened. He inhaled slowly and spoke with controlled indifference. "Aubrey Stewart has every right to think what she chooses to think. I was there and I can tell you Mary Beth Owens was no different than usual."

There! He'd said it! He struggled to keep his cool. He could feel Wade's penetrating stare as the senior detective mentally recorded every word, every gesture, every pause or stammer.

Detective Wade asked, "You saw Mrs. Owens again, on Saturday evening, was she okay then?"

"As I told you earlier, I saw her at Ramsey's house. She was fine. Ramsey was fine. We had a few drinks. I went home."

"Did they ask you to stay for dinner?" Detective Wade asked.

"Yes. I declined."

Greg pressed his palms against his thighs, drying them on his trousers. If Detective Wade or this Stokes kid wanted to shake his hand, he wanted to be ready. He needed to get these guys off his back.

Detective Wade stood and thanked Dr. Palmer for his time.

Once outside, Detective Stokes said, "Am I ever glad I was taking notes when he said they had asked him to dinner! He sat right there and lied."

"Wait a minute now, Bud. He may have lied. Maybe they changed their minds and decided to cook at home. Maybe he lied, but for other reasons. Let's not get too excited. It's a detail, maybe a detail that matters, maybe not"

What had piqued Detective Wade's interest most about Greg Palmer had been the reaction he displayed to the mention of Aubrey Stewart's name. Detective Stokes had briefed him on his visit to the hospital to question Aubrey Stewart.

"Did Mrs. Stewart have much to say about Dr. Palmer?"

"Only in reference to the conversation he had with Mrs. Owens on Friday morning," Detective Jon Stokes answered.

"Do you have Mrs. Stewart's home phone number on you?" Detective Wade asked Detective Stokes as he glanced at his watch.

"Yes sir," he said.

Detective Wade picked up his mobile phone and punched in the number as Detective Stokes called it out to him.

"Mrs. Stewart, this is Detective Sam Wade of the BVPD, I was wondering if I could ask you a few questions about Mrs. Mary Beth Owens."

"I spoke with a Detective Stokes today about the case." Aubrey was half asleep as she spoke.

"Yes ma'am. I'm his partner."

"Detective Stokes didn't tell me to expect a call from you," Aubrey added suspiciously. She sat up in bed and rubbed her eyes.

"Could you hold a minute ma'am?" Detective Wade asked.

"Yes," she answered.

"Jon, ah, Detective Stokes would you please tell your friend, Mrs. Stewart, that it's okay for her to talk with me," he said, shaking his head in amusement.

Detective Stokes took the phone, "Mrs. Stewart, this is Detective Jon Stokes. I spoke with you this morning at the hospital. Detective Sam Wade is my senior partner; he is working with me on this case. Would it be possible for us to drop by for a minute?" He spoke, prompted by Detective Wade. Detective Stokes was about as puzzled as Aubrey appeared to be as to why Detective Wade felt it necessary to talk with her tonight. Then he recalled his partner's question referencing Dr. Palmer and Mrs. Stewart.

Aubrey said it would be all right and gave Detective Stokes her address. *"This will save me a call,"* she thought.

She looked at the bedside clock, eight-fifteen. She barely had time to get dressed before the doorbell rang.

"Hello Mrs. Stewart, it's good to see you again. This is my partner, Detective Sam Wade." Detective Stokes spoke as he came through the doorway.

"Sam Wade, hello ma'am." The detective spoke as he entered, his broad shoulders practically filling the door frame. Aubrey took his extended right hand and apologized for being cautious on the phone.

"No need to apologize, ma'am. We should apologize for our intrusion. Thank you for seeing us."

Aubrey nodded, looking up to Detective Wade and continued to stand in the entry.

"Is it okay if we sit in here?" Sam asked as he motioned toward the spacious living area, fine wrinkles appearing around his gentle eyes as he smiled.

Aubrey blushed with embarrassment, "I'm so sorry. Please forgive me. This whole thing has been so awful I barely know who I am." She put her open hands out toward them and spoke, "Let me put some coffee on, and you both come in here. We can sit at the table or the bar, wherever you're more comfortable." That said, she led the two detectives toward the kitchen.

The telephone rang. Aubrey excused herself and answered the phone, busying herself with the preparation of the coffee as she talked.

At Douglas's suggestion, their son would be staying over at his place. Eric called to say goodnight. The attentiveness of this Douglas was a welcome change from the Douglas of a few months ago. Aubrey had noticed his kindness toward her, though somewhat superficial, had been freely offered over the last few days. He no longer avoided her. Their wounds were healing; now kindness sat where passion had lived.

Aubrey carried a tray holding three cups and saucers, cream, sugar, and coffee to the table. Over the business of serving, she noticed the senior detective studying the cover of her copy of Dame Juliana's *"A Treatyse of Fysshynge wyth an Angle"*.

"Fysshynge," he said, extending the s sound, his bushy black brows pushed together as he squinted at the book title.

"Oh," Aubrey explained, "Fishing, in Middle English, I think; I suppose they spelled things more phonetically in the 1400's. I like reading through it, the bits of wisdom and everything about fly fishing, from how to make your own rod from a tree branch to the behaviors of a noble sportsman.

"Philosopher, fishergirl, well, she probably would have called herself an angler, and published author, that's being accomplished," she said, opening her hands out in amazement.

Detective Wade returned the book to the table and commented on Aubrey's frequent use of hand gestures, as he took the coffee Aubrey offered.

"Everyone tells me I couldn't talk without my hands, but since I've been learning to tie knots for my line and tie my own flies for fishing, I sometimes occupy my hands by practicing tying knots." She sipped her coffee and added, "I'm sure you didn't come over for me to tell you all this. Thank you though, for the distraction!" She smiled and nodded toward Detective Wade.

"Now, how may I help you?"

"Actually, ma'am, we came here to clarify a few things," Detective Wade spoke with authority as pulled a dog-eared notepad from his jacket pocket. "We're sorry to burden you with more questions. It's just that we are trying to figure out exactly what happened and who, if anyone, is accountable."

"Mrs. Stewart, you told Detective Stokes," Detective Wade said nodding toward his junior partner, "That you were concerned about your nurse friend, Mrs. Owens. Can you explain why?"

Aubrey drew in a deep breath and began, "I hope I can. In fact, I was going to call you first thing in the morning," she said, directing her last comment toward Detective Stokes. She started by detailing what she had witnessed in OR Ten and Mary Beth's unnatural demeanor in the locker room. Detective Wade nodded and she continued, "Mary Beth had me thinking Dr. Palmer had done a trach, a simple procedure. A part of me did believe her, but her explanations were too canned; she had reasons for everything, it all seemed too logical. Also, she had been anxious to leave and excused herself by saying she had to drop the specimen off at Pathology.

"As I left the hospital, not more than five minutes behind her, a man at the loading dock handed Mary Beth an envelope and pushed what looked like a big box into the back of a van. I watched him drive away, not bothering to switch his lights on until he had driven halfway down the block." While recounting for the detectives her last encounters and conversations with Mary Beth, Aubrey clasped her hands, momentarily forcing them into her lap. She thought that these two were probably thinking she was totally ditzoid. Detective Wade listening intently as Detective Stokes busily assumed the role of scribe.

Directing her words to Detective Stokes, she said to him, "I must apologize to you for my vagueness this morning at the hospital. Until this afternoon, I tried to believe that Mary Beth had been right and that I had misjudged the situation. Ethics and honesty used to be non-negotiable for Mary Beth." Detective Stokes adjusted his collar as he gestured an approving nod toward Aubrey.

"Today, I discovered the patient who Dr. Palmer operated on Thursday night died during the procedure. I firmly believe that the patient's organs were harvested." Aubrey couldn't think of a way to prove this bold accusation. The patient had been brain-dead, and death during the procedure might not be considered an untoward event. His body had been cremated: no corpse existed to prove a violation had occurred. The person she had confronted was dead, so Aubrey's story was just that, a story.

"How did you come across this information about Dr. Palmer's patient?" Detective Wade asked.

"My routine paperwork hit a snag. To resolve the discrepancy, I reviewed the patient's chart and discovered, quite by accident, the patient's family had refused organ donation. Dr. Palmer had stayed with the patient until the personnel from the funeral home came for him. The deceased was to be cremated. I mentioned it to my director today because Dr. Palmer usually delegates every task he can, yet he chose to spend an hour or so in the OR with a corpse."

"And all of this is unusual?" Detective Wade prodded.

"It is for him. Well, to be absolutely fair to him I should say it seemed out of character for Dr. Palmer." Aubrey placed her thumb against her little finger and said, "To appear to be so attentive to the family, to talk with them about organ donation, to be so detailed with his progress report, and, especially since it was so late, (with this, she pinched her index finger against her thumb, spreading her hand open) to actually wait and sign the body over to the personnel from the crematory, that's not the Dr. Palmer I know. All these tasks he could easily assign and usually didn't waste a minute in doing just that."

"Sorry to interrupt, what do you mean, 'talk to the family about organ donation'?" Detective Wade asked.

Aubrey explained that state regulations mandated that the next of kin always be offered the opportunity to donate organs or tissue. A signed organ donor card or anything short of absolute refusal is delegated to procurement specialists who visit with the family, address any concerns, and determine the feasibility of donation.

"It is protocol, just not something I would imagine him doing. Sometimes they can't use the organs, even if the family does wish to donate."

"So, this patient dies. There's a chance he could have been an organ donor, but Dr. Palmer talked to the family and they didn't want to do consider that route?" Detective Wade furrowed his dark brows together as he translated the information Aubrey reported.

"That's what he wrote in the progress record. And that, in and of itself, is not unusual, except he was not the primary physician. Ordinarily, the primary physician would take the initiative in these matters and contact the procurement team. Dr. Palmer likely asked the parents prior to the procedure, which is a matter of routine. Generally, the surgeon lists all the potential complications, including death before the operative permits are signed. It would have been entirely appropriate for him to address organ donation again at that time. What appeared out of place to me was his attentiveness after the procedure. Dr. Palmer handled it all himself, in the middle of the night. This is the same doctor who has to be caught to sign off verbal orders during the day. The body was never even brought back to the ICU. Practice varies a bit, yet Blakely policy directs that the body of a deceased patient not be left alone in a room or unit. Instead of taking the deceased patient back to his room in the unit where the nurse assigned to the patient would have remained at the bedside until the personnel from the funeral home arrived, Dr. Palmer stayed with him until he was received by the crematory attendants.

"It's all rambly and disconnected, I know. I'm trying to make some kind of sense of it myself. Since documentation states Dr. Palmer's patient expired during surgery, I'm positive that what happened Thursday night in OR Ten was an unauthorized harvest. In fact, a planned, unauthorized harvest." Aubrey's eyes focused on the notepad in Detective Stokes's lap.

"I know this is very difficult for you, Mrs. Stewart, but if you don't mind, I have one more question. Can you tell me how you would describe your relationship with Dr. Palmer?" He wanted to know what fueled the apparent animosity Aubrey and Greg had for one another.

"Strictly professional," Aubrey responded without hesitation. Then she described Greg as a demanding, self-serving doctor. "He insists on having his own special instrument trays. Once, a circulator pulled one of his trays for an ENT case with another surgeon and he stormed into the OR director's office screaming as though his personal property had been stolen. Of the twelve board certified anesthesiologists, Dr. Palmer has approved only two to be posted with him for the surgical schedule. Since one of them is over sixty and not required to take call, that left only Dr. Pate to be on call with him. Also, he has alienated most of the other staff members. Just the other day he requested Mary Beth and one other nurse be the circulators assigned OR call when he is on call. I don't know who he is going to find to work with now," her voice faltered.

"The only interaction I have with Dr. Greg Palmer is professionally at Blakely, nothing more," Aubrey concluded as she cradled her cup in both hands and sipped her coffee.

"We've kept you too long," Detective Wade said. "You need to rest. Don't try so hard to figure things out. That's our job. Right, Jon?" He spoke kindly, smiling toward Aubrey. Then, cocking his head toward Detective Stokes, he said, "He and I will take all the information we have and do our best to decipher it."

Detective Wade glanced down at his watch, mostly to avoid facing the despair in Aubrey's wet blue eyes.

"I thank you, Mrs. Stewart. Now, it's time for us to leave you alone so you can get some shut eye. Anyway, we don't want to wear out our welcome the first time we're here," Detective Wade spoke as he stood to leave.

Detective Stokes rose, following Detective Wade's lead and added, "Thanks for all the information. Goodnight ma'am."

Aubrey leaned against the door after she had turned the deadbolt. No matter how foolish she appeared to others, she felt relieved for having voiced her impressions. She had the compelling notion Dr. Palmer stayed with the deceased patient and signed the body over to the crematory for reasons other than kindness. Ramsey and Mary Beth were the two people who knew his reasons, and they were dead.

Outside, Detective Stokes cleared his throat and paused, hoping Detective Wade would break the silence. With no such luck, he offered, "Well, what did you think?"

Detective Wade said, "I'm not sure. She could be running on emotions. You know, dead friend and no explanation for it." He climbed into the car, turned the ignition and shifted into gear as he continued, "Our sweet Mrs. Stewart thinks Dr. Palmer is a bad guy. Being a bad guy doesn't make him responsible for the deaths of her friends. Does makes you wonder what the doc has been up to." Detective Wade seemed to be talking to himself.

"It is our job to determine if any evidence exists to substantiate her claims. We can add a possible harvest to our list of possible scenarios. How's that for a can of worms, Jon?"

Chapter Twenty-Four

Tuesday afternoon the security supervisor was waiting when Aubrey arrived.

"Thank you for seeing me." She had called on Monday, leaving a message to arrange a meeting at their mutual convenience.

"Glad to help. You had a question about a Patient Occurrence Memo?"

"Yes sir," Aubrey nodded as she answered. The memo had been the only angle she could think of that might help her discover what had taken place in OR Ten. Aubrey had filed it on Friday afternoon.

Sitting at his desk, he turned a logbook around so Aubrey could see the entries. "All Patient Occurrence Memos come here first; this department stamps the original with the date and time received, makes a copy, which is sent to the department head where the event occurred, and forwards the original to the Quality Improvement Committee. It took us awhile to get all the departments to cooperate. Some of them wanted to do their own fixing, that way they could turn in perfect scores. With this system, they're obligated to address it properly and the Quality Improvement people can make recommendations, check again, whatever." Using a ballpoint pen as a pointer, he directed Aubrey's attention to a line near the top of the page where her memo, or POM as it was called, had been received.

"Your director should receive her copy today, tomorrow at the latest. House mail can be slow at times, but your memo is in the system." His chair groaned and creaked as he leaned back, his fingers laced and bowed, at the back of his head drawing attention from his twelve pack abdomen to his chest and thick upper arms.

Aubrey applauded his ability, "You have so many areas under your command and still manage to keep up with all the ins-and-outs of the operation," and then, as she was about to present her second petition, his offer saved her.

"Anything else I can help you with?"

"As a matter of fact, I am rather interested in how the surveillance cameras work. You know the post anesthesia nurse is sometimes way back in there alone and the doors are open. It can get kinda spooky. If something were to happen, could you call up dates and run tapes from the cameras, after the fact?" Aubrey wanted to validate what she had discovered in the patient record.

"That's one thing I can say for Blakely. If it's state of the art, we buy two. Let me show you." The Chief Security Officer of Blakely Hospital rose from his chair and escorted Aubrey to the area where two switchboard operators sat, responding to flashing lights, beeps, and made overhead announcements; and, a security guard, dressed in khakis and a white shirt, the sleeves rolled up to mid-forearm, slurped on a red straw stuck in a large Styrofoam cup, as he held vigil over a wall full of monitors displaying a kaleidoscope of pictures. A navy blazer decorated with a badge on the left chest pocket hung on a coat rack in the corner.

"Ryan, this is Aubrey from the Recovery Room, show her how we can review the film."

The slender young man straightened in his chair and started to explain how the system archived film. "Pick a date," he said.

"How about last Thursday night? That's the night I was on call." After he had the department data entered, Ryan entered the date and film started to roll.

"There I am," Aubrey said as she watched a black and white movie of herself pushing the patient stretcher in the hall. "Can you show more, like around the halls and outside?"

Ryan scanned as he spoke. "They record clips at set intervals and, in certain areas, when the motion detector is activated. Like in your department, when security makes rounds and locks up, the Same Day Surgery cameras go off until the next morning. Mrs Krantz figured that one out; it saves some money."

He paused, "Here we go." The monitor, listing the date and time in the lower right corner, showed a man in scrubs, Dr. Greg Palmer.

"He's always a jerk." Ryan didn't have any interest in watching Dr. Palmer walk down the hall, but his curiosity did pique when he saw a man pushing a stretcher covered with a burgundy velvet drape come around the corner.

"That's the guy from the funeral home. He must have made a wrong turn." Ryan scanned footage of the doors covering the ICU, then concluded the guy had gone down the OR corridor for a body. "Yep, there's Palmer going out behind him."

"Proof, for all the good it does," Aubrey thought, as she watched.

"How long have we had this system?" Aubrey asked, intrigued with this technology.

Ryan tapped his fingers against the edge of the desk, keeping time with the background music. "About two years, in most of the departments. Your super, Ms. Krantz, got all bent about patient privacy being jeopardized, you know, in gowns or half-naked, so it took a little longer before that got settled, but not more than a few months."

Aubrey wanted to ask about the surveillance cameras at the loading dock. However, hesitant to raise questions with further probing, she thanked the guard and excused herself.

When she left work for the day, she exited the door that she typically only used when she left the hospital after hours, the same door she had passed through when she was on call the previous Thursday. She paused for a minute to survey the area. The loading dock was empty. Would Mary Beth have told her what Dr. Palmer did in OR Ten that night if they had met for dinner before she died? Was it the reason she was dead? A cold dread surged through Aubrey's entire body. Why was she the only person to think that the fire had not been an accident?

As she opened her car door, Aubrey looked across its roof and caught sight of a car stopped at the corner. It idled at the empty four way stop sign a bit too long. As Aubrey watched, the man drove slowly toward the hospital. She felt his eyes burning into her as she hurriedly climbed inside her car and locked the doors. The ten seconds or so it took for the diesel's amber glow plug to go off so she could crank the engine seemed like an hour; at times like this, she needed a gas burner. Glancing in the rearview mirror after she turned the corner, she sighed with relief when the car did not follow her.

Once home, she checked to see that all the doors and windows were locked. Eric was supposed to go to Douglas's after school. Aubrey called to make certain he had arrived safely.

Sitting in the kitchen, she glanced through the headlines in the newspaper while enjoying her tea and the tea cakes Mrs. Leland had made. The only item concerning the deaths of Ramsey and Mary Beth was a tag line at the end of the long list of obituaries listing their names and stating their funeral arrangements were pending. Drawing warmth into her fingers as she cradled the bowl of the teacup, a near palpable sadness overwhelmed Aubrey.

She had the phone in her hand to call Mary Beth's parents' home, when she decided to pay them a visit instead.

Sarah, Mary Beth's older sister, answered the door. Aubrey followed Sarah through to the living room.

"Have a seat," she ordered, and then added, "I'll get us something to drink. As she left the room, she said, "Mother and Daddy have taken Cassie and one of her friends out for burgers. I told them to go see a movie, anything to keep them from sitting around here. I don't know how long I can just wait for something to happen."

Sarah lived in Dallas, where she had recently been promoted to Chief Financial Officer for a large oil firm. She seemed to be living up to her reputation as a take-charge sort of person, but she found this new unknown factor too enigmatic for her checks and balances type life.

Listening to the whir of the ceiling fan and the barely-audible dialogue from a TV in a distant room, Aubrey watched as Sarah poured tea from a carafe and handed her a glass. Sarah resembled Mary Beth, not entirely, but they shared the same auburn colored hair and complexion. Sarah looked taller than Mary Beth. They may have shared an identical gene pool, but they had entirely different personalities. Mary Beth was reticent and submissive, while Sarah personified boldness.

"Howie's back in the den, knocked out. Not drunk; in fact I think this is one of the few times I've seen him sober." Sarah didn't mince words about her sister's ex-husband. She had often referred to Howie as, "One nightmare away from a dream come true."

"Is there anything I can do?" Aubrey lamely offered.

"Thanks, not now. I don't know what to do myself. I have to sit her and listen to my parents while they worry out loud. It's crazy." Sarah looked directly into Aubrey's eyes and added, "Aubrey, it's been, what three days, and we haven't heard a word. Well, they said they're searching through everything. So far, nothing to try to match with their dental records." As soon as these words left her lips, Sarah lowered her head and cried. Aubrey moved over to sit beside Sarah and stroked the back of her hand, a hand so like Mary Beth's.

"Mary Beth once told me about your sewing project for Home Ec," Aubrey said.

Wiping her eyes, Sarah looked over to Aubrey and said, "She would have remembered that. Yeah, I should have selected a sleeveless shift like the other girls. I had to pick that long-sleeve, fully-lined, lavender, wool dress with a cowl neck, cuffed sleeves with buttons, and a fitted waist." Sarah's face softened as she reminisced, "Mary Beth had the patience to rip out the seams I had put together backward, or whatever. If I could have afforded, I would have bought more fabric before I would sit and tweeze out all those little lavender stitches. What a mess I gave her, but she turned it into a pretty dress, and I made an A. Well, if Mary Beth told you the story, then you know she earned the A.

"It's weird to remember things like that and not be able to remember the last time I told her I loved her." Sarah stared at the carafe and empty glasses on the coffee table, where a late afternoon sun poured through the window and livened the crystal with white stars. "More tea," she asked Aubrey.

"I've had enough, thanks," Aubrey said.

Back at home, Aubrey sat, enjoying the memories of her friend's bright face, when the vision of the desperation in Mary Beth's eyes on Thursday night returned to haunt her. Aubrey closed her eyes, trying to visualize the stranger who had met Mary Beth at the loading dock. Her memory couldn't capture any details about the man, but she did recall the box the stranger heaved into the van. It had not been a box at all, but a large ice chest.

Human organs were placed in a saline bath, the bag then packed in ice and put in an ice chest for transport. Aubrey remembered this from her ICU days.

Staff RNs and graduate nurses were required to work one year in the ICU before they could be considered for transfer to the PACU. During Aubrey's year in the ICU, a young woman had been admitted with a ruptured cerebral aneurysm. After it had been determined she would not recover, her parents nobly decided to donate her heart and kidneys. The ventilator had kept the patient's organs oxygenated until the harvest team arrived. Aubrey received permission to observe the harvest. The details of that day were forever crystallized in Aubrey's mind.

The halo of brightness on the surgical area intensified the paleness of the slender body lying on the operating table. Her chest and abdomen, prepped and bisected with a cauterizing scalpel, lay open as the pungent odor of searing flesh wafted through the surgical masks and lodged in the nostrils of those in the operating room.

After the invasive grind of the saw, as it split the sternum to open the chest, the voice of the anesthesiologist emphasized the gloom as he announced the patient's vital signs with a sober cadence. The kidneys were harvested first. Then, honoring the donor, the team of surgeons, the anesthesiologist, circulating nurses, and three surgical assistants, paused as the girl's pastor, wearing surgical gown and mask, made a step forward and commended the young woman's soul to God.

From the corner of the room, Aubrey gazed as a surgeon cross-clamped the artery at the top of the heart. The wall clock pointed both its long, black fingers straight down. Time had ceased for the patient. While retractors kept the ribs spread, Aubrey watched as the surgeon severed the vessels between the clamps and lifted the fist-sized heart from the chest cavity. The organs, packed in a slush of iced saline, were labeled and readied for transport. Two members of the harvest team left the OR with a white ice chest.

Her hands trembled as she noisily sat her cup on the saucer. The eighteen-year-old young man who died that night would have been the perfect candidate for organ donation. A massive head injury had rendered him brain-dead. However, according to Dr. Greg Palmer's progress record, the patient's family had declined to talk with anyone about the possibility of donating his organs.

Aubrey pieced together all the evidence. That night in the locker room, Mary Beth had said, "He was brain-dead," not is, but was, and the man at the loading dock pushed an ice chest into his van. Dr. Palmer had stayed with the patient and signed the body over to the mortuary to guarantee no one would discover a harvest had taken place. He had used OR Ten so that the equipment for opening the chest would be accessible.

It made perfect sense. *"So what went wrong?"* Aubrey wondered what could have happened to cause Mary Beth and Ramsey to get murdered.

Until she had enough evidence to convince Rebecca that Dr. Palmer had taken part in a stealthy harvest, Aubrey needed to keep quiet. The Patient Occurrence Memo she had initiated had to be intercepted.

When she had filled out the form, she reported observing Mary Beth functioning as the circulating nurse, and as the scrub tech. By policy, in on-call situations, the minimum staff, other than surgeon and anesthesiologist, should include a circulating nurse and a scrub tech, or a surgical assistant. Rebecca, as department head, would receive the memo. Her first move, in resolving the occurrence, would be to confront Dr. Palmer with the document, informing him of Aubrey's observation of him in OR Ten. Aubrey wasn't ready to be Dr. Palmer's next victim.

The afternoon interdepartmental mail went to the surgical desk in the inner corridor. Springing from her chair, Aubrey glanced at her watch. It was five minutes before six. She dialed the direct number for the surgical area. No answer. The staff would be changing into their street clothes.

Chapter Twenty-Five

Mrs. Stewart had looked toward his car far too long. Mitchell slowly pulled away from the stop sign and drove past the parking lot where she routinely parked. He watched while her back was turned toward him to be positive she got into the car. After her back up lights flashed on, he turned right and circled the block, keeping his distance. Her car, more noticeable than most because of the occasional gray burst of diesel smoke from the exhaust, signaled to him like a beckoning flag. Mitchell could spot Mrs. Stewart's car a mile away. He kept her in his sights and watched as she turned off Highland. When he arrived at the alley drive, Mrs. Stewart pulled in to her driveway. She didn't deviate from the route she had taken on Monday.

Mitchell looped back toward downtown and the doctor's office, making a quick pit stop for gas and a sandwich. With the cops swarming around, he had to keep his distance. This afternoon he parked diagonally across the street from Dr. Palmer's office so that he could see the office doors and spot the doctor's car when it left the parking lot. From this position, he could ease away from the curb and fall in behind Dr. Palmer without being noticed. The doctor never took the direct route; he wasn't as predictable as Mrs. Stewart.

Chapter Twenty-Six

When Detective Wade arrived back at the station, he found Detective Stokes sitting at his desk reading Dr. Palmer's statements, scrutinizing every word.

"Bud, it's a whole 'nother world over there," he said, bringing Detective Stokes up to speed about his trip to the hospital. "They're all running around in these blue scrubs, just like on TV. You can't tell the janitor from the brain surgeon. They talk in abbreviations or acronyms I've never heard before. Like our lingo is strange to civvies, they have their own 'medicalese.' This patient had a 'Lap something,' or that one is having PVC's and we need an EKG STAT, I know that one from the television. Most of it's like a foreign language.

"They're like a football team, everybody in uniform, they huddle over the patient before they go into action, and then each person does his job. Mrs. Stewart is certainly in her element there. I didn't want her to get all emotional again, thinking about her friend, so I told one of the nurses just to tell her 'hello' for me."

Detective Wade continued, "I did confirm some of Mrs. Stewart's notions about Dr. Palmer with the nurse who arranges for organ donations. I was directed to her office from the Medical Records Department. I had gone there first to see if I could take a look at the chart of that kid Palmer operated on last week. I told them I just wanted to confirm the doctor's statement about his working relationship with Mrs. Owens and Dr. Pate. I signed their paperwork showing which chart I wanted, but the chart wasn't in the department. The clerk there sent me to the office of Diane Reynolds, the coordinator for the organ donation program. The chart had been sent to her office. Apparently she reviews the charts of all deceased patients.

"She thought it was a little unusual that Dr. Palmer had been so courteous to the family. She explained that the neurologist had taken a long weekend, and he left Dr. Palmer in charge of the kid. According to her, Dr. Palmer may have simply taken his obligation seriously. Possibly because the other doctor was depending on him. Whatever his reason, every "i" had been dotted and every "t" crossed. There doesn't appear to be any suspicion about the case on that end.

"If you want to know anything about organ donation, well, Mrs. Reynolds can tell you. Take the kidney: thirty thousand people are on the list, in this country alone, for a kidney. The average wait is over a year. Over a dozen people die every day waiting for some kind of organ transplant. Can you imagine? And they use it all. Heart and lungs together, now that's a major thing. But for the heart and lungs to be transplanted together, they must be taken from the donor and stuck directly into the recipient. They have to be in adjoining operating rooms. They can't have any lag time for that kind of operation. Too many minutes without oxygen and the lungs are useless. Kidneys can be out of the body for up to twenty-four hours before transplanting.

"In some countries you can walk in and sell one of your kidneys. Bet you didn't know that. Here everything has to be donated. A friend or family member can be checked out to see if he is a match, and if he is, he can donate a kidney specifically to that person. You can't sell an organ, and you can't buy your way to the top of the list if you need an organ."

Detective Wade hadn't given much thought to the needs of patients with organ failure until he had visited Mrs. Reynolds. The reality that many of these people died while waiting for a replacement organ caused him to sympathize with the plight of the patients and their families. He thought about the terminal wait for a donor organ compared to the last ditch hope for a cure by a person consumed with cancer.

"Here." Detective Wade handed him a red bean shaped sticker that read 'I love you with all my kidney.' "They give these out to make people aware of the organ donor program."

Detective Stokes took the sticker, inspected it, then placed it inside his desk drawer. Detective Wade examined his junior partner's desk. He picked up a form. It had been neatly placed on the right side of the desk. Except for the telephone, the report he was reading, and the legal pad Jon was jotting notes on, it was the only thing on top of the desk.

"How do you keep your desk so clean?" Detective Wade asked Detective Stokes. His own desk was a collection of stacks of folders with ragged edges and note pads. One stack precariously topped with a coffee mug, likely as not containing yesterday's dregs.

The younger detective only shrugged and gave Detective Wade a half smile as he looked toward the disarray on his senior partner's desk.

Sam read the form. "Have you heard any word on 'Hair, unknown source' you sent to the lab in San Jacinto for analysis?"

"Nada," Detective Stokes sounded defeated.

"At least it's something Bud. Remember, attention to every detail of your actions can keep you from screwing up, and that same attention to every detail of a case might uncover the other guy's screw up." Detective Wade's encouraging voice sounded genuine. "Let's go out there and see if they've been able to sift through the mess." He didn't intend to put a damper on his fledgling partner's investigation by telling him the sample he sent would probably turn out to be a dead end.

"First, I want to run something past you."

"I'm all ears," Detective Wade finally sat down.

"Mrs. Owens's locker at the hospital was empty, except for a few personal hygiene products, and her house was neat too, no notes scribbled on things anywhere. I thought maybe she was one of those clean-slate types. The only thing in her trash was the start of a note to Mrs. Stewart; just the salutation.

"I didn't think too much of it at the time, but when I peeked into her attic, I found boxes and boxes full of old schedules. Not very organized, but she did have a system. Printouts of the daily surgical schedule, folded, with notes about patient procedures, supplies needed to restock operating rooms, patient room numbers, phone numbers, appointments for the orthodontist and to get her hair highlighted, mortgage refinance rates, and anything that she needed to remember, were all bundled by the month. Names were blacked out with a check mark and time, I guess the time the case ended, or with a red 'CX,' obviously that's for a cancellation. Years and years of the stuff; I'm talking the stuff dates back to when I was in junior high, each of the bundles covered two, sometimes three months. Sam, every month was up there except April and May of this year."

"And they weren't anywhere in the house?" Detective Wade asked.

"Nowhere. With that kind of order for all those years, she should have had at least a week's worth in her locker and a stack somewhere in the house."

"Do we know who had access to her locker? Or if she locked it routinely? Since their dressing room is in a secure area, they may not bother with locking up their belongings," Detective Wade added.

"Her supervisor, Ms. Krantz opened it for me Monday. It was locked at that time. I called and was told she couldn't see me today; I've made an appointment to see her tomorrow afternoon at four."

"Good plan. Reckon something was written on one of those papers we weren't supposed to see?" Detective Wade asked as he stood.

"Or, someone may have thought so, you know taken them from her locker just in case. If she was up to anything, it would be on that schedule. She could have taken those schedules and filled in the gaps to write her memoir." Detective Stokes said.

Detective Wade took the passenger seat, "You drive, Bud." Detective Stokes backed out of a space marked, "Reserved."

"Do you think they've found any long bone fragments, anything, maybe teeth or jewelry, something that could confirm the two of them were there when the house burned?"

"It would be helpful to have evidence of a corpse when you can't have the real thing, wouldn't it now? Sometimes, well, often in the real world, you just have to settle for 'likely'," Detective Wade said.

Chapter Twenty-Seven

Aubrey pushed a stack of unopened mail toward the console between the seats and climbed into the passenger side of the Jeep. "Thanks for picking me up, Judge. I didn't know who else to call."

"Anytime. Tell me again, what is this conspiracy all about?"

"The other day, when I thought you were a real judge, I had wanted to ask about the obligation to report something I saw in the operating room. I had sent a memo concerning the staff involved, as a way of opening the case for review, since the nurse had tried to convince me that the surgeon had done a trach, a relatively simple operation, and, as much as I wanted to believe her, I sensed there had to be more to it. Well, yesterday I discovered that I had witnessed an unauthorized harvest of organs. I didn't actually see the harvest, but I'm certain that's what happened. Mary Beth Owens was the nurse and Ramsey Pate was the anesthesiologist for that case. Now they're dead."

"The house fire?"

"Yes, and I believe the surgeon is responsible for their deaths. I mean, how likely is it you do something illegal and two days later you die?"

He didn't respond but mulled it over as he continued to drive. At the hospital, Aubrey pointed, saying, "Pull in over there by that car," directing him to the space nearest the entrance by the Same Day Surgery elevator.

"I shouldn't take more than ten minutes," Aubrey said as she grabbed at the door handle. She nudged, then pushed the stubborn door with her shoulder.

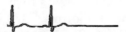

Aubrey entered the empty locker room and slipped a set of scrubs on over her street clothes. She tucked her hair into a surgical hat. Instead of changing shoes, she pulled a pair of shoe covers over her sandals.

The corridor connecting the PACU with the OR was dark. Aubrey stayed to the side and eased around to the inner corridor where light spilled from an open door. She waited for a minute. With no indication anyone was in the room, she went to the desk and pulled the wire basket marked "In" onto the counter. Several interdepartmental envelopes were in the stack, all addressed to the OR Director. Aubrey pulled the string, of the first, unwinding it from the button closure. A bid from a vendor for new equipment was enclosed. The second and the third envelopes held bulletins about conferences. Aubrey unwound the forth envelope and found a memo concerning the sterilizing equipment. She would have to check again tomorrow.

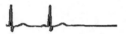

"Aubrey, what are you doing here so late," the voice called out as she walked toward the Jeep.

Without pause, Aubrey jerked at the door of the Jeep before she turned to address her colleague. "I forgot to pick up a memo. I called to save myself a trip, but all of you late nurses had left."

"I grabbed a sandwich from the cafeteria. There's a hot appendix coming in from the boonies. They should hit the ER in a few minutes."

"Maybe that will be your only case and you can get home before bedtime. See you tomorrow," Aubrey said and waved goodbye.

The male nurse stared at the judge and Aubrey as the Jeep heaved its way onto the street.

"We need a faster getaway vehicle if we intend to make a habit of this. That guy had enough time to sketch a picture of the Jeep," the judge said.

He held the steering wheel with his left hand and rooted around in the cup holder with the other, finally extracting a couple of candies. He offered Aubrey one.

"Do you eat at "The Olive Garden" every day, or do you steal these mints?" she asked, as she ripped away the green foil and shoved the soft chocolaty mint into her mouth.

"The hostess likes me," he said. Then added, while savoring his mint, "I might be stepping past my bounds, but a straight arrow dame like you shouldn't be running around trying to put out brush fires. You could get yourself in a tight spot and you wouldn't know how to fight back."

"I'll be all right, Judge. Dr. Palmer didn't see me up there."

Chapter Twenty-Eight

Since the judge had declined Aubrey's offer to cook dinner as a thank you for driving her to the hospital, she sat with a cup of tea and watched the last half of the news until the telephone demanded her attention.

"Mrs. Stewart, this is Sam Wade. I'm in your neighborhood. I thought I would stop by if it's all right with you ma'am."

"Sure, that's okay. I need a few minutes to get myself together. Is there something new?"

"Nothing earth shaking. But then, I haven't called it quits yet. How about ten minutes? I'll drive the limit."

Aubrey rushed upstairs. She splashed cool water on her face, slapped on some lipstick, combed through her hair, and gathered it into a pony tail at the nape of her neck. When the doorbell rang, she had just stepped off the landing.

Detective Wade arrived carrying a big white bag. "You won't tell anybody that I had bourbon sauce on my bread pudding while on duty, will you?"

Aubrey had to smile. "Not if you share. I'll make us some coffee."

He opened a carryout container and poured the bourbon sauce into the small glass pitcher Aubrey offered him. "You've had this before," he said, as she heated the sauce in the microwave.

"River Pearl is one of my favorite places," she said. Remembering her last conversation with Mary Beth, she wondered if her friend would still be alive if she had taken her up on the invitation to dinner there Saturday night.

Aubrey's eyes, full with tears, focused on the microwave oven's blurred red flashing numbers, as the seconds ticked away. Suppressing the impulse to share with Detective Wade the details of her trip to the hospital, she opened the cabinet and removed two dessert plates as Detective Wade proceeded to tell of his discovery.

"Jon and I went to see Mr. Pate today, and we drove to his son's house. He told me all about how Ramsey and his first wife had it built. It's on the back corner of Mr. Pate's property. That's why Dr. Pate paid through the nose twice to keep the house. Neither of his exes particularly wanted the property; according to Mr. Pate they had been city girls. Do you have an ex, Mrs. Stewart?"

"Douglas and I aren't married anymore. Would you call him an ex?"

Detective Wade cleared his throat and looked directly at Aubrey, "I'd call him crazy." Then, without blinking he added candidly, "I reckon he still qualifies as an ex though."

As the slightest smile tugged at the corners of her mouth, Aubrey turned around and busied herself setting the table.

He filled the two cups Aubrey had placed on the counter and brought them to the table while he continued to tell her of Mr. Pate, whose only child, Ramsey had died.

"He told me he lost the only thing he valued in this world. He has nothing left. His wife died when Ramsey was a teenager. Poor old guy; just won't let go. And, he refuses to believe the hot water heater could have caused the fire."

"I agree with him," Aubrey said. "I mean, how could something that holds water start a fire? It doesn't make sense."

"The fire marshal says the hot water heater could be the possible source. The heater had been installed in the garage against the interior wall. Evidently if a gas leak exists, the gas will accumulate in a low, dark area. The arc created when a light switch is flipped has potential to ignite an explosion capable of setting a fire. The switch plate beside the door from the garage to the den was only a couple of feet from the hot water heater. So, all those factors do make it possible. Whether that particular sequence of events actually caused the fire, I don't know that anyone will be able to prove."

Detective Wade continued, "Anyway, here's this little old gray haired man, lean and strong looking for a man of his age, wanting to see what's going on and at the same time trying to stay out of the way. Standing there hoping for answers. He's so alone. Frankly, I was glad they didn't find anything while we were there. He perked up ready to go the minute I asked if he would like to join Jon and me for something to eat." Detective Wade smiled, shaking his head at the thought of Mr. Pate.

"About the time we crossed the cattle guard to leave, he told me to backup. I put the car in reverse and backed over the cattle guard and had started to make the turn toward the house when he bailed out of the car," Sam said indicating his surprise at Mr. Pate's action.

"He shot out of the car and headed back toward the entrance before I could get the car in park.

"I thought the old guy had lost it. Then he said, 'I told Ram this was a foolish waste of good money but he bought it anyway'. All this time, he's pulling loose bricks out from one of the columns at the entry. Then, his hand popped out, clutching a security camera. The system had been programmed to buzz in the house if a vehicle came onto the property through the entry and the camera had been set up to snap a picture of anything that crossed the cattle guard.

"Mr. Pate said his son only turned it on during deer season. The doc had installed the system after he had problems with hunters coming onto the property uninvited because he feared a stray bullet from a deer rifle might hit someone. On the off chance he did leave it on all the time, we hauled it in for the guys in the lab to check."

"We already know Greg Palmer was there, maybe the last one there," Aubrey said. "Do you think the camera got a picture of his car?"

"We'll see," Detective Wade looked away as he lied to Aubrey. He had seen pictures of a van leaving in the dust trail of Dr. Palmer's sports car. He also had seen pictures of the same van making another trip in and out after dark.

"The crime lab has it and they will have a complete report tomorrow evening, if not sooner. Jon spotted a reporter hanging around across the road, watching every move we made. I'm sure he will push for the scoop, and, as a man of my word," he said, cocking his head toward Aubrey, "I wanted to share our news with you before you read about it in the paper."

"I appreciate that," she said, convinced there had to be more information that he did not have the liberty to share. Before he left, Detective Wade promised to keep her apprised of any developments.

The palest orange ribboned evening sky reflected the setting sun's rich color from under a canopy of deep blue as Aubrey looked out the bedroom window. She shed her sleeveless top and capris and crawled into bed exhausted only to be wakened moments later, or it seemed, by someone banging on the front door.

Karen and Barbara burst into the house. "You should have called us. We could have come home early." Karen spoke as she hugged Aubrey. Without bothering to inhale she continued, "You look a mess. Get upstairs and splash some cold water on those red eyes and for God's sake, take that holey old robe off. Haven't I begged you to rip it up and make a bathmat from the best pieces if you can't stand the thought of getting rid of the raggedy old thing. What if you died with that awful thing on?"

"Thanks for the comforting thoughts," Aubrey sobbed.

"She didn't mean die, like die." Barbara interjected. "I declare Karen, you need to put this stuff in the kitchen." She ushered Aubrey toward the landing. With her left hand urging Aubrey forward, Barbara moved her right hand across her mouth as her eyes locked with Karen's big blue stare.

Later, with Aubrey dressed in a presentable pair of pajamas, the three friends sat together at the table. Aubrey assured them she had eaten, but encouraged them to eat the pizza they had brought.

"When I talked to Mary Beth Saturday, I didn't think it would be the last time, ever." Aubrey told her friends of what she had seen in the operating room and the encounter at the loading dock on Thursday night. The wine had opened the emotional control gates. She began to cry again.

"Honey, you just cry. It'll do you good." Barbara held to the belief that doctors should prescribe chocolates and therapeutic crying instead of antidepressants. "You were close to her, working with her everyday. Why, it's a shock to us and we only knew her through you. I'm sorry we didn't know to get here sooner. The minute I pulled into the driveway Bill stuck my suitcase in the hall and told me I should get over here. He saw Douglas at lunch yesterday. They sat at the same table at Rosa's. Douglas told Bill you were pretty upset about it all."

"Does that mean he's no longer with the squid, or whatever you call her?" Karen asked between bites.

"That's octopus, Karen," Aubrey said. Her lips curled up at the edges. "They are still an item."

"Octopus then, all those arms wrapped around him. He'll never get loose. Didn't you say they have three hearts? What does she say, 'My hearts belong to you.'?"

"She's more likely to give him one and save the others for someone else. That would be justice served," Barbara announced as she lifted the plates from the table.

Karen leaned across the table, her mouth like a horse rejecting its bit, "Have I got anything on my teeth?" Barbara reached for her glasses and held them up to her face, squinted, then shook her head.

After they had run themselves down, a contented quiet enveloped the three for the first time since Aubrey's friends had trooped in with carry-out pizza. Barbara poured more wine into the glasses.

The aroma of chocolate filled the kitchen. "Which of these coffees should I make," Karen asked? She stood with the deep cupboard drawer open, surveying an assortment of coffees.

"The Goldcoast is my favorite to have with a dessert," Aubrey moved to the counter and pulled out the grinder.

"Goldcoast, she says." Karen checked the labels on the bags. "Why on earth does it make a difference which coffee goes best with chocolate when you sit there and sip that Lambrusco like it's some rare vintage?"

"You only drink the bitter, expensive stuff because some foreign guy at the wine tasting told you it complimented the boldness of tomato sauces, or whatever. If he told you my Lambrusco cost a hundred dollars a bottle, you'd say it had an interesting bouquet and left your pallet tingling with pleasure."

As the lively banter rekindled, Aubrey warmed in this comfortable cocoon. For the first time in days, the rawness of sorrow was soothed.

"You haven't even touched your brownie," Barbara noticed.

"Detective Wade, one of the investigators, came over earlier and brought bread pudding from River Pearl. I'm stuffed"

"I never heard of a detective bringing food, not even the ones on TV. What's this guy up to?" Karen asked, tilting her head to one side.

"I'm certain it's not what you think," Aubrey replied. "He might think I'm crazy from the way I've been behaving. Actually, he seems really interested in finding out exactly what happened, like the detectives on TV."

"Does he think the fire was an accident?" Barbara asked.

"I don't think he has ruled out anything yet."

"If they had committed suicide, they would have made plans and left letters. I saw a movie about this couple, they couldn't be together, I forget why, but I think the man couldn't get out of his marriage, or maybe both of them were married, anyway, they wrote long letters, I'm telling you I sat there and boohooed when they wrote the letters because the movie showed them writing the letters and reading them as they went along, but they mailed the letters, went to this tall bridge, stripped off naked, and jumped in the lake. Now, I wouldn't do that for a man."

"And we're glad," Barbara laughed.

"I'm just saying sometimes people feel trapped. They don't really think things through. You know their kids and family had to watch them get drug out of the lake, naked and filthy, just like big ole fish," Karen said.

"Karen, that was a movie; this is reality. Murder suicide is too messy. The police would be able to figure that out in no time. Anyway, I think they were murdered," Barbara said. Then she offered her own views on the matter, "It has to be murder because they got that heart for some big shot millionaire and once the guy had his heart, he had them murdered so they would never tell."

"That's a good theory, Barbara, but what about Dr. Palmer?" Aubrey asked.

"He's from California. He probably does that kind of thing all the time," Karen interjected.

"I declare, Karen you have had too much wine. Aubrey, it's your fault for letting her have a glass of wine," Barbara said, grabbing Karen's glass, as Aubrey leaned back on the sofa laughing.

Chapter Twenty-Nine

Aubrey stepped out of the shower and grabbed her robe. While blow drying her hair, she thought she had heard the telephone ringing. It had rung late last night, also. By the time Aubrey had awakened enough to answer, the caller hung up. Now, it rang again. She turned the dryer off and headed toward the telephone on the other side of her bed. The ringing stopped the instant she picked up the receiver. Again, the caller disconnected.

She called Douglas. Kimberly answered. Douglas had left for the day. Aubrey declined Kimberly's offer to leave a message. She asked whether Douglas or Eric had called late last night.

"Why? Is there a problem?" Kimberly politely asked, her words popping forth, like air bubbles.

"No, everything is fine. It's just that I missed two calls and wanted to make certain Eric hadn't needed me," Aubrey answered. She silently chastised herself for having called this husband-stealing invertebrate.

Kimberly's high pitched rhythmic assurance that Eric was fine and Douglas had left for work failed to comfort Aubrey. She then offered her condolences and her 'heartfelt sympathy' for the loss of Aubrey's friend and ended the conversation with a salty, "Take care, dear."

Aubrey thanked her with what graciousness she could muster and hung up the telephone.

When Douglas had first moved out, she had checked all the windows and doors every night to make certain they were all securely locked. Lights came on and went off randomly throughout the house by means of preset timers. A pair of Douglas's old, size-twelve loafers, by the back entrance, warned potential intruders of a man's presence. If she heard an unfamiliar noise, Aubrey surveyed the entire house. By now she should have adjusted to Douglas's absence. The paranoia had to stop. Eric was getting older. She would be alone more often, and she couldn't be suspicious of every wrong number.

Armed with this self-addressed counsel, she took her cup and saucer to the sink, rinsed the cup, and turned it upside down on the saucer in the sink.

One look at the rose stem she had placed in a clear glass of water beside the sink revealed the cutting hadn't yet decided to live. Following the specific directions of Mrs. Leland, in this third effort, Aubrey had carefully pulled the small branch from the main trunk of her Peace Rose. An entire new rose bush could be started from this severed branch, if it took root. Aubrey searched for signs of root development each day as though the appearance of a budding root would somehow, in the cosmic order of her universe, bear evidence that she would survive independently without the security of an intact nuclear family. The stem remained green; there was still hope. She picked up her backpack. Her hand was wrapped around the door knob when the telephone rang again.

"Hello," she answered, suspicious already. Her resolve had lasted only about ten minutes.

"Mrs. Stewart, are you all right?" It was Detective Sam Wade.

"I am," she said in relief. "Thank you. I was just leaving for the hospital."

"That's the reason I called. I'm going to be at Blakely today. Do you mind if I stop by your department? There's something you might be interested in. I promise I won't bother you if you're busy."

"I'll look forward to it." Aubrey replied.

Detective Wade's comments puzzled her. Had he discovered something through his investigation that proved Ramsey and Mary Beth had been murdered or was he patronizing her? Aubrey's interest piqued; she wanted to know what Detective Wade had to share.

Chapter Thirty

The chief had allowed Sam full reign in his investigation, with the caution to keep a low profile. Sam had positioned himself at the corner nearest the entrance of the cul de sac where Aubrey lived. From there, he could see if anyone went down her street or into the alley. He had watched two females leave about midnight, probably the friends Mrs. Stewart had mentioned.

Sam stretched, as much as the confines of the driver's seat of his standard issue Ford sedan would allow and readjusted his seat before he fastened his seat belt. His eyes had grown heavy from lack of sleep. After watching Mrs. Stewart drive out of her alley and turn toward Highland Street, he pulled away from the curb.

At the hospital the day before, Sam had been especially careful not to indicate that he had any suspicions whatsoever about Dr. Greg Palmer. He made his visit to the Medical Records Department with the pretext of confirming the work relationship Dr. Palmer shared with Mrs. Owens and Dr. Pate, which in part was true. His second motive had been to gain information about organ harvest. The black market for human organs was big business. Sam knew all too well if money was involved, the door to corruption was open wide.

The second funeral home Sam called on had produced a Disposition of Body form, signed by Dr. Greg Palmer, authorizing the funeral home to cremate the patient, an eighteen-year-old male. Dr. Palmer was the only person alive who knew if his deceased patient had left the hospital with all his organs intact.

The pictures of a van taken by the camera mounted beside the cattle guard at the entrance to Ramsey Pate's property provided tangible evidence that Dr. Greg Palmer had not been entirely truthful. Palmer had neglected to tell them that someone else was at the Pate house on Saturday evening. Yet, a van followed him out of Ramsey Pate's driveway. Sam reckoned Dr. Palmer had an awful lot at stake to keep the identity of the van driver a secret rather than have an iron clad alibi. If he had left Mary Beth Owens and Ramsey Pate alive and well as he had said, he should be glad he had this witness to confirm his claim.

The news of the security camera would become public knowledge this morning, likely making the front page of The West Texas News Aegis. Those who were on the film knew who they were and Sam was certain things would start happening very soon, and he had an obligation to protect Mrs. Stewart.

Sam drove slowly, keeping enough distance behind Mrs. Stewart to avoid being noticed. After she entered the hospital, he drove himself home.

Once home, Sam slung his coat and tie across a chair and headed for the kitchen. He needed to be sharp today and there was no time for a nap. He methodically measured two full scoops of coffee beans and put them into the grinder. He held the button down while he timed the grinder for fourteen seconds. Then he spooned the ground coffee into a filter in the top of the coffee maker. He rinsed the carafe, filled it with cold water to the eight cup line, and poured it into the reservoir. While the smell of fresh coffee drifted across the kitchen, Sam shaved and showered.

Chapter Thirty-One

The instant Greg slid into his car, his car telephone rang. "Hello," he said. A cold dread enveloped him when he heard the voice of the caller.

"Where are you, Greg?" Mitchell asked.

"I'm driving to the hospital," Greg answered, knowing fully that Mitchell probably already knew his exact location.

"Have you seen your morning paper yet?"

Greg's paper was likely still on the front step. "No," he said. "Why, what's in it?"

"Just a tidbit about the, 'On going investigation into the fire and probable deaths of prominent local physician and his fiancée.' Security camera may show who was at the Pate house on Saturday night.' Dear old Dad says his son usually only checked it during hunting season." Mitchell conveyed the news to Palmer as he had been directed. Obviously the group had someone monitoring all the events in Buena Vista. Vince might still be in town.

Greg's tie was choking him. He loosened it. His heart pounded. "Mitchell, what if they saw you and Vince and that other guy there? How are we going to explain? What are we going to do?"

"They didn't see me there, and you didn't either. You say nothing. You do nothing. The camera may have been turned off.

131

This may be a bluff. Stay close to your phone. I'll call later." He hung up.

Greg Palmer's response to the news was as predicted by the group. Vince had been notified of the discovery, but no one had to remind Vince he should stay alert. That soldier didn't make it home from the desert by being asleep at the wheel. If a camera did exist and the van was spotted, there would be an all-points bulletin on it before the day was out.

Greg nervously looked around as he drove to the hospital. He didn't notice anyone following him. Parking in an end position next to the building, instead of his reserved space, he glanced around the lot before he got out of his car. Thankful he didn't meet another doctor or staff member that he might feel obligated to pause and chat with, he entered the hospital. He didn't have anything on the surgery schedule. Wednesdays were his half-day office days. The morning was usually spent making rounds at the hospital and catching up on paperwork. He made rounds in record time and appeared busy when anyone looked as if they wanted to talk.

Leaving by way of the stairs, he paused only to nod and mumble a quick 'morning' to the few fellow doctors he did encounter. He didn't bother to acknowledge the other staff members and visitors he passed. Safely back in his car, he sat a moment before backing out.

He entered his office building through the back door and went to the reception area. He told his nurse he wasn't to be disturbed. She always honored his request for privacy, except in the case of dire emergencies.

In the confines of his office, he locked the door and leaned his head back, eyes closed. Both hands were behind him, gripping the cold doorknob. The scent of his new leather furniture drifted into his nostrils. He could barely breathe. His heart pounded in his chest. Greg knew with all certainty that Mitchell and Vince would be untraceable. He also knew that, if the camera had been turned on, the police would ask him about the van.

Greg didn't want to tell them the truth. He wasn't even sure of the whole truth. Thankfully, he didn't know details, but he was certain that if Ramsey and Mary Beth were dead, he would receive full blame.

Chapter Thirty-Two

Detective Wade checked in with his partner. "What's up, Bud?"

"Nothing unusual. Dr. Palmer went to the hospital. Was in there about forty minutes. Straight to his office. He's in there now.

"He did talk on the phone most of the way to the hospital, the best I could tell.

"What I did see was another car drive past the Doc's office. He has circled the block twice. I called in the tag numbers. It's a rental to some medical sales group. Maybe just a sales rep making rounds, but he drove past two vacant parking spaces."

"So, that's why you're hiding out here in the bushes. Smart lad," Sam said, catching a glimpse of Jon's car as he was driving down the alley toward the doctor's office. Instead of pulling over to the back of the patient parking lot, Sam stayed in the parking lot of the pharmacy across the street. He positioned his rearview mirror in order to keep an eye on the back entrance of Dr. Palmer's office.

He assumed the surveillance position and sent Jon for a break.

"Be back in an hour," he said. "I want to get to the hospital by lunch."

Sam added, "Don't make a big deal about what we're doing. Remember, we don't want anyone to think that the fire was anything more than an accident."

The chief didn't want any negative publicity to come from this investigation. He had told him, "Sam, I'm depending on you guys to stay out of sight. It's bad enough to have one of the community's doctors dead; we surely don't need the whole town to think one may be a murderer. The kind of trouble you are talking about could cause us a lot of grief. If the news hounds get scent of what you are doing, they'll have a field day."

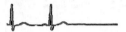

Sam knew all too well about their lack of regard for privacy. He had lost his temper with a reporter after the initial investigation of a fatal car crash. The driver of a pickup reportedly ran a red light and plowed into a high school senior and her prom date. All three involved were pronounced dead at the scene.

A reporter had witnessed Detective Wade being led away from the wreckage by a uniformed officer. Back at the station, before the identification of the victims had been made public, the reporter insisted on knowing why Detective Wade was escorted from the scene and if he had been taken into custody. Sam overheard the guy and bolted through the door and slammed the reporter against the wall, but not before informing him it was none of his business. Two uniformed officers stopped him from hurting the guy. Sam's act of rage on the night his niece was killed haunted him for some time. A cop wasn't supposed to have emotions.

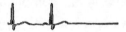

He didn't want to cause a stir. However, he could think of only one reason Dr. Palmer would fail to mention the fact that someone else was at Ramsey Pate's on Saturday night and that was, if the other person presented more of a threat to Greg Palmer than being suspected of arson and murder. Detective Wade's intuition told him that tailing Palmer would pay off.

Chapter Thirty-Three

Three nurses stood over the bed of the patient being admitted to the PACU. Aubrey gently lifted his head to pull the elastic band of the oxygen mask behind his head.

"Your surgery is all finished. You're in the Recovery Room. Can you take a slow, deep breath for me?" She wished she had a dollar for every time she had said, "Take a deep breath."

The patient groaned and grimaced, "It hurts."

The anesthesiologist removed a blunt cap from a syringe and injected the clear liquid contents into the intravenous line. "That's another fifty mics of Fentanyl." He discarded the syringe into the sharps container.

The patient in slot five was connected to the monitors; the heart rate, respiratory rate, blood pressure, oxygen saturation, and temperature were all documented by the anesthesiologist and the PACU nurse. The primary nurse completed her assessment and covered the patient with a warm blanket.

The patient had undergone a simple hernia operation. The endotracheal tube was still in place. His respiratory effort remained extremely weak, necessitating manual inflation of his lungs with an Ambu bag on transfer from the OR. The anesthesiologist squeezed the large blue bulb slowly, delivering oxygen to the patient's lungs until the ventilator was connected. The nurse placed the diaphragm of her stethoscope against the patient's chest and listened for breath sounds. Ventilated breaths were now pushing oxygen into his lungs. The patient did not respond to his name or the vigorous rubs on his chest by the doctor. A quick review of the case notes indicated the patient had been given a reversal drug to counteract the muscle relaxant that he received before the incision was made; therefore, paralysis was ruled out. He had also received a dose of narcotic at the end of the case. Not a large dose. Narcan was administered intravenously to reverse the effects of the narcotics. The patient's status failed to improve. His heart rate and blood pressure remained stable. Blood samples were drawn and sent to the lab. The patient was transferred to the Intensive Care Unit.

The remainder of the cases were admitted and dismissed uneventfully. Aubrey directed her attention to the stack of mail on her desk: a vendor's price quote for a piece of equipment, a flyer announcing a nursing conference, and an interoffice correspondence envelope. Aubrey stared at the envelope bearing Aubrey's name in the 'Forward To' column. A small pink sticky note plastered to the middle of the envelope was blank except for a crescent line drawn with a pink highlighter, a faint smile. Aubrey looked around the unit. Who had done this? No one was watching to yell, "Gotcha." She peeled the note away from the brown envelope to reveal another note requesting her to complete the document by filling in the highlighted blank. The space for the patient's chart number had been marked with a yellow fluorescent line. Aubrey wrote, "Thanks to my ghost Angel," on the pink note and placed the envelope inside the top drawer of her desk. Thankfully, she had not had a patient chart number when she initiated the memo; the chart couldn't be pulled and sent to Rebecca, with the Patient Occurrence Memo, unless the requesting document was complete.

She sat at her desk contemplating what to do with the POM when Sam Wade pecked on the frame of the open door with the back of his hand. "Got a minute, ma'am?" he asked.

"I have the rest of the day. Unless there is an add-on, we're finished. Come in." Aubrey stood to greet him and offered him the remaining chair in her office. Once the door was closed, she sat with her back to the outside wall. "Would you like something to drink?"

"No, thank you though." He shook his head slightly as he settled back in his chair. "I apologize for putting you through this, but I need to ask you to recount for me again the details of what you witnessed at the loading dock last Thursday night."

"That's practically all I've thought about this week. I can't get it out of my mind." Aubrey spoke softly. "I was glad to get out of the hospital. I took in a deep breath of fresh air. I guess it took that long for my eyes to adjust to the shadows and the darkness, or maybe it was their movement that caught my attention. I could see Mary Beth. She was talking to a man who had his back turned to me. They were standing at the back of a van. The van doors were open. The man shoved an ice chest into the van. He climbed into the van and drove away. Mary Beth went around toward the Outpatient area."

"Could you describe the van?" Sam asked.

"It was a dark color. The doors opened in the middle," she said as she brought her hands together. Aubrey thought for a minute then added, "The bumper wasn't shiny. It must have been the color of the van. When the doors of the van were open, the inside lights weren't on. I thought that was a bit odd. I don't remember seeing anything inside the van."

Sam seemed pleased with her description. "Does this look like the van you saw?" He asked as he handed her a black and white picture that looked like it had been made on a copy machine.

Aubrey studied the picture. Half the page showed the front of a van and the other half showed the back. "I didn't see the front, but this is like the van I saw," she said pointing to the rear view. Aubrey asked if the picture of the van had been taken by Ramsey Pate's security camera.

"Yes. It was. Now I just have to figure out who it belongs to and why it was at Dr. Pate's house Saturday night," Detective Wade said. Aware the pictures weren't the best pieces of evidence, Sam eagerly accepted whatever he could to tie the two incidents together, no matter how weak.

"I have a theory," Aubrey said. She was interrupted by the telephone. "Excuse me," she said, picking up the receiver.

"Yes, hold on please," Aubrey handed the phone to Detective Wade. "Detective Stokes wants to speak to you."

"Sam, sorry to bother you, but this is urgent. Can you break away and meet me at the station? There was a call from San Jacinto. The chief has asked to see us. He sent a patrolman out to relieve me."

"No problem, Bud. I'll be right there."

Sam handed the receiver back to Aubrey and said, "I'm sorry I can't stick around, but duty calls." Detective Wade was gone before Aubrey had the opportunity to mention her suspicions concerning Dr. Palmer.

Valerie waved, motioning for Aubrey from the desk in the center of the unit. Aubrey went to the desk to investigate.

"The patient that was in five, Dr Peterson thinks his pseudocholinesterase levels are subnormal. Results aren't back yet." Typically patients were given an intravenous dose of succinylcholine, a paralyzing drug which wears off in five to ten minute, to facilitate the placement of the breathing tube that ventilates the patient's lungs during surgery. Most people naturally produce the enzyme, pseudocholinesterase, which reverses the effects of the drug. This patient might be one of the very few persons who did not produce that enzyme, or had very low levels. If so, he would require ventilator support for breathing overnight.

"Can you imagine the ICU?" Valerie said, not expecting an answer. "Patient doesn't wake up after surgery and there's no explanation for it and their big concern is filling in all the blanks! They called over here wanting to know his weight. Like it's not written on the chart. Did they think his weight was going change with a hernia repair?"

Valerie continued to talk, but Aubrey had stopped listening. She had just experienced an epiphany. She stepped into her office and looked up the number of the crematorium.

She explained that she had been completing records for a quality improvement study and needed the weight of a patient who had expired and had been sent there for cremation. Without hesitation, John, the manager on duty, had checked the record and had given her the information she requested.

She dashed downstairs to Medical Records and signed the log as required when requesting information and recorded the number of the chart she needed.

"You're in luck!" the clerk said. "I was going to file this. It just came back to the department today."

"Thanks! I won't take but a minute," Aubrey said as she glanced at the chart. There they were; his daily weights, recorded every early am, as the patients in ICU were routinely weighed between midnight and four in the morning. She handed the chart back to the clerk and thanked her.

The four pound discrepancy wasn't much, but it just might be the ammunition she needed to convince someone to believe her. The patient had weighed one hundred forty-eight pounds every day for the eight days of hospitalization prior to his death. When the crematory had received him, he weighed one hundred forty-four. She didn't intend to address the notion that different scales could constitute a variable. That would have to be proven. It did sound too bizarre to happen at Blakely: stealing the organs of a human and selling them.

Listing the facts as she sat at her desk, Aubrey turned to see Rebecca in the doorway. "I saw Detective Wade in the hall. If he gets pushy asking too many questions about Mary Beth and Ramsey, you have every right to ask him to leave you alone."

"That's not a problem. Actually, he seems more interested in this case than I thought he would be," Aubrey said. "I still believe they were killed and I want to know why.

"Rebecca, think about it. There's no way they would've died in a house fire. They could have easily escaped injury. Through the patio doors, through a window." She was on the verge of explaining more of her theory when she noticed all the color drain from Rebecca's face.

Aubrey stared as Rebecca grabbed onto the edge of the desk with her hand and dropped into the chair facing Aubrey. Rebecca's composure had completely disintegrated. As she struggled to find her voice, her eyes darted back and forth, avoiding contact with Aubrey's startled gaze.

She cleared her throat before saying, "That's nonsense. Aubrey, the police said it was accidental. Let them put an end to this mess. In fact, Detective Stokes is coming in at four; I suppose it's for some sort of wrap up session. We need to get it behind us. Remember the hell we went through when Sharon Crawford decided to overdose in the Operating Room? The hospital took a lot of flack trying to keep her little secrets out of the spotlight. We don't want to go there again."

Aubrey turned in her chair and moved her arm to cover the list she had intended to share with Detective Wade.

Recovering enough to paste an almost convincing smile on her troubled face, Rebecca continued, this time with her usual authority. "You're not thinking clearly, Aubrey. Maybe you need to go home and take something so you can get some rest. Look, I'll ask Dr. White to order a sedative for you. Time and rest is what you need. This accident has affected all of us; Mary Beth and Ramsey were like family to most of us."

Fearful of further confrontation, Aubrey nodded toward Rebecca in agreement.

"You're right. Nothing is going to bring them back. Mary Beth and Ramsey weren't just my friends, they were your friends, friends to everyone here; it's selfish of me to continue this search for answers." Aubrey hoped her response to Rebecca's rebuff had sounded convincing.

"Stop by my office on your way out." Rebecca said. Recomposed and in charge, she left the unit.

Chapter Thirty-Four

Mitchell had tired in his efforts to maintain continual surveillance on Palmer and keep tabs on Mrs. Stewart at the same time. No sooner had he followed her home than he had to get back downtown and hope that the doc had not left his office. When he did have a spare minute, invariably a call would come in with a message for Palmer or instructions for himself or Vince. This watch and wait game had grown old.

Mitchell watched a patrol car ease into the parking lot across the street. Deliberately, he drove in the opposite direction to avoid detection. Picking up his car phone on the first ring, his contact from the group identified himself with the usual, "How's the weather," then asked if Mitchell saw anything. Mitchell reported the police car in the doctor's parking lot.

Detailed instructions were laid out as Mitchell felt his heart race with a rush of adrenaline. It was about time he got a little action.

His old man would have a conniption fit if he knew the truth. The major thought junior managed the security department of a global corporation. Mitchell's tense facial muscles relaxed into a smirk as he thought of the family patriarch, the chest thumping warrior who had practiced his interrogation techniques on his kids all those years. Those days were long gone. Nobody pulled Mitchell's strings anymore.

Mitchell focused on his assignment. Thinking through the plan as it had been outlined to him. He considered the consequences of a snag. If stopped with the purse or other valuables of this woman, he would be the only one implicated; this bothered Mitchell. He had always covered his tracks. He didn't intend to be caught with anything that could be traced to the victim.

The plan described to him purposefully mirrored the MO of an intruder terrorizing women in the Austin area. Supposedly, the guy operated alone: His targeted victims single working women who lived in the suburbs. The crimes occurred immediately after the women arrived home, indicating the guy had followed them. Or, he somehow was familiar with their routines. Suspected of having committed several rapes with robbery and one murder, this perpetrator had not been apprehended.

Calculating his risks, Mitchell determined the best thing to do was to refrain from telling his contact with the group that he had no intention of being caught holding the bag, literally. Instead he would put the stuff in an envelope addressed to the Post Office Box the group assigned him, and then he would ditch the key. If they wanted the stuff as evidence, they would have it. If he were to be arrested, the group would be accountable, even if indirectly. Mitchell called Vince to relay the instructions he had taken for him. A recorded message came on. "The customer you have called has turned the phone off or has traveled out of range. Please try your call again later."

Chapter Thirty-Five

The station was less than a mile from Blakely. Detective Wade pulled into the first empty parking space he found and started into the building when Detective Stokes caught up with him.

"The chief called and said a detective from San Jacinto had some questions about the sample I sent. He said something about it being a positive match."

Sam gave Jon a proud nod as the two went directly to office of the Chief of Police. Chief Dan Thurman sat waiting for them. He motioned for them to have a seat while he fumbled with his reading glasses. With the glasses perched low on his nose, he commenced to brief them on what he had learned.

"The lab in San Jacinto identified the sample you sent as a human hair.

Turns out it's a positive match to the hair sample of a woman who has been missing for a couple of weeks. The victim was a twenty-two year old woman who had moved to the area the previous month. She and her roommate and a few friends had gone to the Riverfront to eat. Julie Carlisle, that's the victim, excused herself to go to the bathroom and never returned. Her friends became concerned when she failed to rejoin them. They called the police. Several eyewitnesses saw a man lifting a woman, fitting her description, into a van. One of the witnesses stated the man made a comment about his girlfriend having had one too many margaritas. None of the witnesses recalled anything significant about the man or the van. One man "thought" the van had Texas license plates."

"The investigators in San Jacinto had taken prints and hair samples from Ms. Carlisle's apartment so they could check them against Jane Does. They hadn't had a single lead until today. When the hair matched the sample you sent, they wanted to know all about where it was found and any leads we have. I gave them what information we have on the Owens-Pate case. The mention of the van generated a great deal of interest. According to their reports, the witnesses' descriptions of the van, as vague as they are, match the images we have of the van as it entered and left the Pate house."

The chief looked at Detective Stokes, "Exactly how did you come across that sample you sent in?" Giving the young detective his full attention, he leaned forward, his chin in his hand.

"I spotted it down in an opening by the driveway. It looked like something that had been stuck in a vacuum cleaner tube, swirled, perfectly round. I could tell it was hair; jet black and long. Mrs. Owens had auburn hair. There wasn't any dirt on it. I figured it hadn't been there long. That little curled up bit of hair was the only thing I could find that appeared out of the ordinary."

The young detective reasoned, "If the van had been parked with the rear doors toward the garage, the sample could have fallen out and blown into the crack where I found it."

"Well, kid, looks like you hit pay dirt. Good job." The chief smiled and nodded toward the blushing detective. He continued, "They issued an APB on the van. A Ranger stopped a man driving a black van on Interstate 10 at the Junction exit. The driver's name is Vince Colsten. He's a vet with a clean record. He did let the Ranger look inside his van. The thing is decked out like an ambulance. The guy said he had bought it from an ambulance service and had plans to renovate it and make it into a little motor home for himself.

"A used ambulance with what the Ranger described as, "fancy medical equipment" in it. Do either of you have any idea why this vehicle would have been at the Pate house Saturday night?"

Detective Wade cleared his throat to speak, "A nurse who worked with Mrs. Owens was leaving the hospital last Thursday night and saw Mrs. Owens and a man at the loading dock. The man put something into a van and left. A young man died at Blakely that same night while he was in surgery for a routine procedure. The nurse has insisted the events in the operating room and at the loading dock that night had a direct connection with the fire and apparent deaths of Mrs. Owens and Dr. Pate." He looked at his partner as he continued, "In her statement, Mrs. Stewart told us Dr. Palmer had talked with the family of the young man who died last week and they had refused to have his organs donated for transplant. Mrs. Stewart was suspicious of Dr. Palmer for calling the crematorium and signing the body over to them, instead of asking a nurse to do it. According to her, this attention to detail was out of character for him. She has persistently stated her friend, Mary Beth Owens, seemed to be uncharacteristically troubled."

He paused before uttering his suspicions. The ramifications of such an accusation could destroy his reputation and that of the force if he was wrong.

"Have you heard about the black market for human organs?" He watched the chief's eyes turn to saucers as he continued, "We don't have anything conclusive," Detective Wade said, throwing his hands up. "What we do have is three, maybe four dead people and not one body."

Sam laid out for the chief all the information he had learned about organ procurement and donation and the dire straits of those in need of replacement organs to sustain life.

"Desperation and greed can lead to grievous actions. It is entirely possible the kidneys, liver and heart of that young man were removed and secreted off to Mexico or who knows where. As for Mrs. Owens and Dr. Pate, and now this Ms. Carlisle, they could have been taken to a hospital for organ removal and then their bodies disposed of at the site of harvest. Who would know? We don't have any remains to check. All we have is a picture of a van. You know the old saying, 'one picture is worth a thousand words.' In this case, 'one picture may solve the crime,' at least the picture of the van leaving Dr. Pate's house provides us with a link we likely would never have been able to make."

The chief knew this cockamamie story had to have merit or Sam wouldn't mention it. He now knew why Sam and Jon had wanted to keep a tail on Dr. Palmer. "Then someone needs to visit Dr. Palmer and see if he can remember a few details to add to his statement."

"We could go," Detective Stokes said, nodding toward Detective Wade.

Detective Wade looked at his watch. He had wanted to be at the hospital by four. He had five minutes. "Mrs. Stewart is the only person who can place the van at the hospital on the night the young man died. We need to keep an eye on her. I don't want any of those goons getting too close to her."

The chief noticed the urgency in Detective Wade's voice and interjected, "I could go with Jon, as his backup."

"Good, thanks Chief," Sam said as he picked up the telephone and dialed Mrs. Stewart's unit in the hospital. The nurse who answered said Aubrey had left for the day.

"I've got to get out of here. Bud, you take care of old Dan. He's used to sitting behind a desk," Sam said as he winked at the chief. Then he added, "Seriously, Dr. Palmer is probably playing with some big boys. Keep your guard up." He continued, "Jon, that car you saw cruising past, bring the chief up to speed on it and have someone find out exactly who the driver is and what he's peddling."

Sam dialed Mrs. Stewart's home phone. Then he called for back up.

Chapter Thirty-Six

When Greg had set up his practice in the new office, Leah had presented him with several pictures, mounted and framed in dark cherry wood to go on his desk. He examined the innocent, carefree expressions on the faces of his family. He glanced at the one of himself standing beside his car. The picture then came to him as vividly as the elegantly framed ones before him; Greg had a very definite understanding of how Mitchell had come to know him.

Greg had taken his car to the dealership in San Jacinto for routine service and maintenance. One of the managers initiated a conversation. Greg told the man all about himself, his new practice, his massive student debts, his family, the cost of setting up his practice, the whole nine yards. Information he would not have shared with anyone he knew, he spilled out to this complete stranger. Greg felt a coal of fire growing in his gut. How could he have been so gullible?

He couldn't remember the guy's name or what he had looked like, except he appeared to be an older man, probably late fifties or early sixties, well dressed. Greg had thought he had detected a slight inflection in his voice. He remembered asking him where he was from. The guy hadn't answered; instead, he had changed the subject.

The entire episode had been forgotten, until now. Mitchell and the guy Greg had talked to at the Mercedes-Benz dealership were somehow associated. Greg wondered how he could prove a connection and if there would be any benefit for him to try.

If he sat back and did nothing, this whole thing might blow over. Ramsey Pate had already been the fodder for gossip with his history of narcotic addiction and his numerous romances. Another scandal and Blakely would never be able to shed its soap opera image. A ruling of accidental death would be neat and tidy.

Greg didn't need to call any attention to himself. The best thing he could do would be to stay quiet and let the dust settle, as Mitchell had so forcefully suggested. After all Mitchell needed him as much as he needed Mitchell. At least, Greg wanted to think that was the case. The security camera bit might have been a scare tactic incorporated by Sam Wade.

The telephone on his desk rang one long ring, indicating an inside call. Greg picked up the receiver. "Yes," he said.

"Dr. Palmer, a detective from the police department is here to see you. Jon Stokes is his name. I told him you were very busy."

Greg knew he wouldn't go away. At least it wasn't that Wade guy. "It's okay. Send him in."

"Thank you for seeing me, Dr Palmer." Detective Stokes said as he entered his office, reaching across the desk to shake hands with Greg. Greg didn't bother to rise out of his chair; instead, he nodded toward Detective Stokes and asked, "Why are you here?"

"I wanted to clarify with you something Mrs. Stewart brought up the other day."

Greg had heard all he wanted to hear about Aubrey Stewart and her concerns. "Look, kid, I'm not liable if Aubrey Stewart has issues over the loss of her cohort. It is her prerogative to think what she wants to think. Now, unless you have some valid concern, I have work to do."

"Actually, with all due respect, I do. I wanted to ask you about the van Mrs. Stewart saw at the hospital the other night when you were there."

Greg Palmer swallowed hard. His jaw tightened, and with a trembling voice he spoke, "I don't know what you're talking about."

The telephone pager light went off on his desk. Greg glanced down at the phone. His nurse used this as a signal of a persistent patient or drug rep waiting to see him.

When he looked up, Detective Stokes's eyes were fixed on his.

Detective Stokes pressed on, "Surely you remember it. It was the same van that left Dr. Ramsey Pate's house directly behind you Saturday night. Mrs. Stewart described it to a tee." He leaned in toward Dr. Palmer, "Who was driving the van for you?"

Greg shot back, "No one was driving a van for me. I left Ramsey's house alone. It's in my statement. Read it."

There was a tap at the door and the chief strode into the private office thanking the receptionist for letting him in. "Hello, Dr. Palmer. I'm Dan Thurman. I work with Detective Stokes. Maybe you'd be more comfortable if you had your lawyer present." They didn't want to take a chance on anything he said to later be discounted as having been said under duress.

Greg Palmer sat straight and moved his clenched fists onto his lap. He had to think fast. His eyes darted from one man to the other. If he said he did want a lawyer, he would be admitting guilt, or knowledge of some wrong doing. If he said he didn't need a lawyer, he would be a dead man.

Chief Dan Thurman leveled his gaze on Greg Palmer's face. "We need you to explain, in detail, what went on at the Pate house on Saturday night." Greg Palmer felt a tourniquet squeezing his chest, preventing air from entering his lungs.

Chapter Thirty-Seven

Vince saw the Texas Ranger make a U-turn, bouncing over the rough median strip and creating a huge cloud of dust as he spun around to pull up behind the van. Dialing the one person he had allegiance to, Vince said, "You need to pack up and leave. We don't have jobs anymore. Keep your eyes open and don't look back."

He erased all the numbers in the telephone and then stowed it inside the upholstery of the driver's seat.

The Ranger asked him several questions before he asked to look inside the van. Vince knew he could refuse, but that would only add suspicion. He stepped out of the van and motioned for the Ranger to look inside. He explained he had bought the van with the intention of converting it into a mini motor home. Since it already had a diesel generator attached, he could camp anywhere. He said he was told he could sell the medical equipment in the van for enough to make the renovation.

The Ranger glanced around inside the van and went back to his car. Vince knew his record was clean and the only thing he had to account for was the van. He also knew he could be taken into custody and held for questioning if there was just cause for suspicion. He prayed his explanation satisfied the Ranger.

Tracing anything back to "the group", as Vince had so often heard Mitchell call them, was impossible.

Vince had never killed anyone. But he had transported kidnapped victims, and he had detonated Mitchell's handiwork. If he was detained or questioned, there would be no Mitchell, no group, and no agent to answer the telephone when he called; he would be going it alone. He turned to face the Ranger.

Vince noticed the Ranger trying to avoid staring at his scarred face. The Ranger thanked him for his cooperation and told him he was checking out leads concerning the transport of illegal aliens. Vince nodded at the Ranger, accepting his excuse for stopping him.

He didn't go directly home. Instead he drove to an RV dealership and hung around for awhile, checking out conversions and feigning an interest in self-contained water systems. When the afternoon traffic peaked, he zigzagged toward home, stopping by a mall to buy sunglasses, summer shirts, shorts and sandals. It wouldn't take long for his whereabouts to be discovered. His official address had been listed at the apartment he had kept downtown since he had been discharged from the service. Since his mother had passed, he stayed at the house where he had grown up and rarely ever went to the apartment. Today he made a quick trip by the apartment on his way to the house. He picked up the few things he had there and took the department store tags off his new clothes. He surveyed the generically furnished efficiency apartment before locking the door for the last time.

The house sat back from the road, behind a row of juniper. He drove up the loose gravel drive and parked in the detached garage beside his mother's old blue Benz. Clouds rumbled about, providing short minutes of respite from the blazing sun. Inside, the house was cooler than usual. Vince didn't want to waste any time. Packing the things he could put in a single duffel bag and a carry-on suitcase, Vince readied himself for the inevitable.

Chapter Thirty-Eight

Mitchell failed to get an answer when he called Vince. The phone had been turned off. He would try again later. While maneuvering the steering wheel with his left hand, he used his right hand to lift the loaded gun from inside the hardback book. He had cut away most of the pages in the drug reference book to conceal the weapon.

Driving down Highland, he turned into the alley behind Mrs. Stewart's house. He could see the top of a straw hat moving back and forth on the other side of the fence across the alley from Mrs. Stewart's driveway.

Fully bloomed irises formed a kaleidoscope of color in the backyard. The thick green pointed blades of leaves opened away from the flowers, framing the ruffled blues, yellows, salmons, purples, and an assortment of double colors and, nearest the deck, a single green and satiny black specimen. This beautiful black iris was the newest addition to her garden.

Edna Leland had spent the first eighteen years of her life in West Texas, helping her momma and daddy with the cotton crop from the time she was big enough to drag a bag and help with the picking. The bolls would dry and open to display the snowy white cotton. However, picking cotton was not an easy job. These dried bolls, or burs, had hard, prickly sharp edges. Her parents couldn't afford gloves. Edna's momma would wrap rags around her hands and tie them tight around her palms. The rags helped some, but she still had scratched, bleeding hands by the end of the day.

She had hated crawling along the dusty rows picking cotton in the scorching heat. Some years she had to stay out of school to pick the cotton if the weather didn't agree or her daddy couldn't find any other help. Those times, Edna had to complete extra homework to catch up with the rest of her class. The blisters on her knees and cuts on her hands were reminders of what her momma and daddy preached to her; get an education so you won't have to dig in the dirt for a living.

Edna had picked her last crop of cotton the first year she was in college. She told herself she would be happy if she didn't have to experience anything to do with digging in the dirt as long as she lived. That changed after she retired from the bank. The first year she put out a couple of shrubs and irises. Soon she was active in the garden club and accepting ribbons for her prize-winning irises with the pride of a new mother showing off her baby.

Barely enough space existed between the rows for her to walk and drag the small plastic crate she used for a seat while she 'worked her flowers' with a small stainless steel paring knife. The knife was her most used garden tool. She used it to divide rhizomes and for thinning, to evict weeds, to loosen the soil around the plants, and to cut fresh blossoms to adorn the homes of her friends, as well as her own.

The sound of a car in the alley caused her to shove the knife into the ground beside the satiny black iris. Straightening her stiff back and holding onto her knees as she pushed herself off the upside down milk crate, she let out a long sigh and pushed the loose strands of pale gray hair back away from her eyes and forehead, tucking them inside her hat. Malcolm, roused from his nap by her stirring, waddled off the deck and started off behind Mrs. Leland.

She walked out of her back gate and headed down the drive toward the alley. A dark-colored car eased down the alley. Mrs. Leland was about to ask the tall man driving the car if she could help him find someone when Malcolm started to bark. The man scowled at Malcolm and stopped his car. Mrs. Leland scooped Malcolm up into her arms and went through her gate, slamming it closed before she put Malcolm down. The metal bolt clinked against the latch as someone opened the gate from the outside. She bent over for her knife.

He overtook her in three long strides, one push forced her head into the rock ledge around her flowers. The dog ran to the crumpled heap and whined as he licked at her outstretched hand. The intruder paused as he stood, taking a quick look around. No one had seen him. There was no reason to take the chance of being noticed by firing the gun. It would appear to be an accidental fall.

He left the yard, climbed back in his car and pulled away. He weaved in and out of traffic as he hurried to get back to the hospital.

Chapter Thirty-Nine

Aubrey pushed the remote control to close the garage door behind her even before she turned the car engine off. She thought she had seen a car following her into the alley. She left her backpack in the passenger seat and dashed into the house. Eric wouldn't be home. Douglas was going to bring him home after dinner.

The phone mate blinked insistently. Aubrey pushed the red flashing light to rewind the tape then she pushed the message button. One message had been recorded. Detective Sam Wade's voice didn't quite have the confident drawl Aubrey had come to know. Instead, with apparent urgency, he announced his name and told Aubrey he would "touch base" with her later, then he added a cautionary "be careful."

Aubrey ran upstairs. Her eye caught a reflection of light moving outside. She heard a car door close as she walked toward the French doors to the balcony. She grabbed the phone and called Douglas.

Eric answered, "Hi, Mom."

Unable to disguise her apprehension as she looked out to see the same car she had spotted a couple of days before at the hospital, Aubrey said, "There's a car in the driveway and I'm not sure whose it is." Before she could finish her sentence, Aubrey could hear a grating sound against the metal frame of the garage.

"Eric, is your dad at home?"

"He said he'd be back in time for dinner."

She tried to remain calm, despite her racing heart. "Eric," she spoke in a controlled voice, "Eric, I think someone may have followed me home."

Aubrey continued frantically, "He's trying to get in the garage!" She could hear the door being forced open. Digging past books two layers deep, her fingers traced the cold, slick metal of the barrel of the gun until she could grasp hold of the grip. She grabbed the clip from the nightstand, snapped it into place, and then tucked the heavy weapon into her waistband.

"Mom you've got to get out of the house." Eric yelled into the phone.

"I can't. It sounds like they are already inside."

"You can go out to my tree house. Quick, Mom, get in my closet. There's a flashlight on the floor beside the doorway. Close the door so no one will see you."

Aubrey followed his instructions. As quietly as she could, she pulled the closet door closed until a thin line of light from underneath the door was all she could see. She groped for the flashlight with her free hand and pushed the toggle. Squinting at the sudden glare of light, she directed the beam toward the back of the closet. The flashlight spotlighted a framed, poster size print of a Houston Oilers player holding her smiling, chunky infant son. It sat leaning against the back wall of the closet. Momentarily captivated by Eric's wide-eyed stare, Aubrey recalled the summers she and Douglas had taken him to watch the team during their summer training sessions. Eric had just learned to walk when this picture had been taken.

"Mom, are you there?"

"I'm here, son," Aubrey whispered into the receiver.

Eric, responding to her whispers, lowered his voice. "Move the poster and crawl into the attic."

She slid the poster to one side and crawled through the opening at the back of Eric's closet. She reached back into the closet and pulled the poster back across the opening to the attic. "I'm in the attic now." There were more noises downstairs in the kitchen. Seconds later, the phone line went dead. She laid the phone down and moved the flashlight to her right hand.

The steady pounding, of feet hitting the stairs, hammered into Aubrey's eardrums. She could hear someone running up the stairs. Aubrey looked out into the blackness of the attic. Dust particles, now visible in the light of the single beam from the flashlight, floated aimlessly. Aubrey could see shafts of light coming through the slats on the shutter over the garage. On her hands and knees, she balanced on a board laid out across the rafters. As she moved forward, the flashlight clunked as it hit the wooden plank. Aubrey turned the flashlight off and wedged it inside the elastic band of her bra. She maneuvered her way silently toward the light. The rough wood pushed tiny splinters under the skin of her fingers and knees as she crept through the darkness. Hot, dusty air in the attic hung in her throat.

When she stood, the board creaked under her feet. She gasped and held her breath, waiting, wondering if anyone had heard. When she heard nothing, she grabbed hold of the window and pulled it open. Aubrey leaned forward and peeked out from between the shutter slats. The car was still there. She couldn't see anyone around it. She flipped the latch and pushed against the shutter, which swung open to the outside.

She pulled her dress up and climbed the make-shift ladder rungs mounted between two wall studs beside the window. She swung her legs out the window and straddled a branch of the mesquite tree. The rough bark of the tree scraped the skin of

Aubrey's legs as she pushed herself from the window with one hand and held onto the tree with the other. She hurried to avoid being noticed.

Aubrey shimmied down the branch until she suspended directly over the tree house. Then, she leaned forward, grasping the branch with one hand over the other, closed her eyes, let go of her leg hold, swung around, and dropped into the tree house with a loud thud.

As he sped down the street and turned into the alley, Detective Wade noticed the two unmarked patrol cars, he had dispatched to the scene to cover the front of the house. The car in the driveway matched the description of one Detective Stokes had identified. He calculated each move, reaching across his chest and drawing his gun, while scanning the open garage. Through the half-open back door, he could see movement. Commotion from inside the house forced the tall figure of a man in a dark suit into view. He fixed his sights chest high near the doorway. A crackling flash buried a bullet in the rock wall near Detective Wade's left shoulder. Hunkering down behind his car, he ordered the shooter to throw down the weapon and put his hands in the air. The man ignored him, firing a second time, shattering the windshield of the car in the driveway.

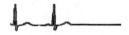

Gripping the gun with trembling hands, Aubrey focused on the motions required. Douglas had told her to pretend the gun was a fly rod.

"In case you ever do have to use it, just think of the barrel as the tip of your rod. Set your sights on what you intend to hit."

Aubrey jacked a cartridge into the chamber before she stood. Taking aim with a broad stance, visualizing her target, the front sight centered in the rear sights, she squeezed the trigger twice then ducked behind the wall of the tree house.

The shooter fell to the ground. One of the uniformed patrolmen leaped through the door and stood with his weapon aimed at the man's chest as a second officer forced the pistol from the downed gunman's grip. With the intruder contained, Detective Wade raced toward the backyard.

Aubrey crouched in the corner, terrified. Steadying the gun with both hands, she held her breath as she heard voices approaching the mesquite tree.

One of the voices sounded familiar. "Mrs. Stewart, Aubrey, it's me, Sam Wade." Aubrey engaged the safety and laid the gun down.

"Your son said I could find you here," Detective Wade said as he climbed the ladder and joined Aubrey in the tree house. "He didn't say you'd be armed."

Chapter Forty

His left hand rubbing his eyes, Dr. Greg Palmer continued to hold his head down as he sat in an orange molded plastic chair at the far end of a laminated wood table. He waited for the door to open and the police chief to walk in as confidently as he had entered his own private office earlier and announce, in his mellow, tone that a criminal had been apprehended and had confessed to the kidnapping and murder of Mary Beth Owens and Ramsey Pate. He also expected to hear them say that all the department needed from him was a brief statement acknowledging his social call on Saturday to the residence of Ramsey Pate, his friend and colleague, and any information he might have that could connect the suspect they have in custody with the fire at the Pate home. After all, there was an election to think of and Chief Dan Thurman might have aspirations for a judge's seat.

Chief Thurman came through the door, but only to escort Everett Drake, the lawyer Greg had asked to be called. Everett Drake was his father-in-law's attorney. Greg had met him at a party soon after he and Leah had moved to town. The two men spoke and shook hands and Chief Thurman left, closing the door on his way out. With his arms folded across his chest, Everett Drake stood looking at Greg, his formidable frame covering the entire doorway.

Without words, Mr. Drake informed Greg of the inconvenience he had caused. He scowled as he selected a chair opposite Greg, throwing his leather satchel onto the table then planting himself on the seat of a reluctant chair. He extracted a yellow legal pad from the bag and pulled a ballpoint pen from his shirt pocket, clearing his throat several times in the process. With nothing left to do, he opened his fleshy red mouth and exposed two rows of yellow stained teeth, worn with age. Greg sat erect in response to the roar that followed as the teeth parted and the lips flapped. The lawyer made it clear to Greg he had come to the station strictly as a favor to his friend, Greg's father-in-law, and by no means was Greg to give him 'a line of crap'.

"Now that the pleasantries are out of the way, I would like you to tell me exactly what happened and why. You may start at the beginning, wherever the hell that is."

Greg looked straight into Everett Drake's steely gray eyes then down at the blank tablet. "It was about a month ago, I was in the waiting area of the Mercedes-Benz dealership and an older gentleman, probably in his late fifties or early sixties, struck up a conversation with me. He was very well dressed in a tailored suit and expensive Italian loafers. It was the typical what do you do, how long have you lived here type chat. I didn't think anything of it at the time; in fact I didn't make the connection until this morning when it all clicked."

Distracted by the sudden thought of the irony of meeting the guy when he did, Greg paused.

"Go on Mr. Palmer. I'm sure this click has something to do with why we are spending the afternoon together in this room."

The sarcasm in his voice caused Greg to shift uneasily in his chair. "Yes sir," he responded, diverting his attention to his own hands. "This morning, as I reviewed every possible connection, it made sense, the conversation in the waiting room. What I took to be a chance, casual encounter was actually an interrogation by him to discover if I would be a candidate to help with his project. It was after this visit, one day when I was driving home from the hospital, that I received a call. The person on the other end identified himself as a friend of a friend and announced the availability of a six figure 'gift' in exchange for a harvest. His exact terminology was, "opportunity to give life by harvesting much-needed viable organs that would otherwise be sent to the graveyard." I didn't realize the opportunity he mentioned would present itself so soon.

"At Blakely, the neurosurgeon was scheduled to be away from Thursday until Monday. Since he is the only neurosurgeon we have at the hospital, the MD on call for the unit would be obligated to cover his patients and any neuro cases requiring surgery during that time would be shipped to San Jacinto. I was on call for the Intensive Care Unit through the weekend. The neurosurgeon's only patient in the ICU was an eighteen-year-old young man who had been in the ICU for more than a week after a motor vehicle accident that left him brain-dead. The EEG showed no brain activity for three consecutive days. His pupils were fixed and dilated since admission to the hospital. He was clinically dead. It was only a matter of time before he was going to be taken off the ventilator and allowed to die. Time for the parents to adjust to the fact he wasn't going to wake up. I had been consulted earlier in the week in reference to performing a tracheotomy, a procedure to insert a breathing tube to ventilate his lungs.

Everett Drake pressed his pen into the paper and underlined the last few words he had written, raised his eyes under the shade of the heavy thicket of graying brows before lifting his head to make eye contact with Greg and ask, "Can you tell me so the ordinary Joe can understand just why you would put a tube down the throat of a dead guy?"

"In this case it was more for the family than the patient. Generally, if a breathing tube has been in the nose or mouth for a week or so, the tissue starts to break down. A tracheotomy, a slit cut directly into the windpipe creates an opening for the tube to be placed there," Greg moved his finger across his throat between his collarbones directly above his sternum, "Once this new airway is established, then one doesn't have to be concerned with the ulceration of the skin and mucosa, that's the inside of the mouth and nose. It buys time without causing problems."

"So, you performed a legitimate procedure even if it was probably unnecessary for this kid. A moneymaker for the hospital and doctors." Drake frowned. "Continue."

"I received a call from the same guy late Wednesday. If I could arrange a harvest, a member of the team would be available to receive the organs. He didn't give me any indication he knew there was a potential donor in the hospital. I don't know if the call was coincidental or he had some information about the patient. Without hospital sanction, I arranged for the organs to be harvested on Thursday night. A member of the team came for transport of the organs; a guy named Vince. I don't know his last name. We were paid with cashier's checks. The checks were issued from trust accounts set up in our names. There were two people from Blakely who participated, Dr. Ramsey Pate and an RN, Mary Beth Owens. They both knew they were part of an unauthorized harvest and accepted compensation for their roles in the harvest."

Greg felt the penetrating x-ray vision of Everett Drake burning into him as he sat at the table examining the joints of his thumbs, not wanting to make eye contact. "Friday morning Mary Beth Owens confronted me in the hospital parking lot. She had been having second thoughts about her decision to participate. I made a date to meet Ramsey and her at Ramsey's house for drinks on Saturday evening. I received a call later on Friday thanking me, and I told the caller about Mary Beth's concerns. I assured him I would smooth things over.

"Without notice, a man named Mitchell showed up at Ramsey's house and had Vince with him. That's when I learned Vince's name. I had never seen either of them before. Mitchell brought a bottle of wine and offered drinks to everyone. After a few minutes, it couldn't have been more than ten or fifteen, Mary Beth paled like all the blood had drained from her body, became very quiet and plopped onto the sofa. Almost immediately, Ramsey grew just as quiet. At that time, Mitchell had me help him to carry both Mary Beth and Ramsey outside and strap them down inside a van. They were like zombies. We strapped them onto stretchers in the cargo area of the van. That was the last I saw of them. I don't know what happened to them."

Pointing toward his notes Everett Drake said, "So we have three enterprising professionals who murder a man for the sale of his organs, two of them have been kidnapped, possibly killed, and one solitary guy is left holding the bag with a story that for all the world sounds like he dreamed it up after watching too much late night TV. Mr. Palmer, you need more than a lawyer, you need a miracle."

Greg struggled to remain composed as Everett Drake continued to slap him with slurs. He wasn't quite sure if the comments were intended to prepare him for the kind of dissection he could expect to endure from the police or if it was merely Drake's way of humiliating him. Greg pretended it wasn't the latter.

"Who else in the hospital would have known of your plans?"

"I'm not aware of anyone," Greg Palmer lamely muttered.

"Do you think it would be fair for me to believe the guys who took Mrs. Owens and Dr. Pate did so with the intentions of killing them for their organs?" With this, Everett Drake's steely eyes steadily drilled into Greg's probing for an answer.

"I don't know. It is possible." Greg did not intend to speculate, with this man, or anyone. So far he was guilty of harvesting the organs of a brain-dead man. He didn't know the law, but that couldn't possibly be as serious as the murder of two people.

Chapter Forty-One

Aubrey watched as blood, her own blood, mingled with the peroxide she used to clean the splintery scrapes on her knees and on the inside of her right thigh. The red ribbon of blood faded to a clear red then iridescent pink as the line trickled down the side of the basin and into the drain. She took the tweezers and carefully excised a splinter from underneath the skin on her knee. She turned off the water to hear voices in the hall by her bedroom. Apparently it was the changing of the guard. Detective Wade had assured her an officer would be staying at the house. Aubrey appreciated the caution. She turned on the shower and tested the temperature with her hand before she removed her robe and stepped into the steamy fog. The warm water pounded on her tense shoulders and aching muscles.

Every part of her body felt sore. She considered herself active. She did her yoga stretches at least four times a week and she still rode her bicycle and played tennis. Apparently none of this had prepared her for the tree climbing experience she had had earlier.

Climbing out of the shower a few minutes later, she dried off, carefully blotting the wounds on her legs and forearms before applying a healthy glob of antibiotic ointment to all the scrapes. She raked through her hair with a comb and wrapped the wet mass in a towel.

Aubrey called out to the officer who was stationed in the hall outside her bedroom. He pulled the door closed so she could get dressed. His uniformed presence validated the reality; she had been within minutes of being the next victim of those awful goons who were responsible for the disappearance and likely death of her friends.

Voices, mingled with the sound of kitchen cabinet doors opening and closing, reverberated up the stairs. She opened the bedroom door and paused, waiting for the officer to go down the stairs before her. Arriving at the foot of the stairs, her face beamed with a radiant glow as her son ran toward her. "Mom, you did it," Eric said with pride. "I was scared you wouldn't get out in time. The 911 operator kept asking me where I was and I kept trying to explain where you were and that I knew someone was there to kill you."

Embracing her son, Aubrey's eyes stung with tears. "Thank God you did. You saved my life."

Douglas stood at the kitchen sink showing Kimberly how to rinse the teapot with boiling water. He turned his head and spoke to Aubrey. "We came over to make sure you were going to be all right, not that you need us after doing so well on your own, along with the backup support of Eric." Eric stood straight, his chest out and his shoulders broad, as he helped his mother into a chair at the table. Douglas taught Kimberly to brew tea while Eric examined Aubrey's wounds and discussed with her the easiest and least injurious way to crawl from the window into the tree.

"Shall I toss this in the garbage?" Kimberly asked Douglas, as she held a dry-looking stem that Aubrey had placed in water by the sink.

"No, please. That's a cutting from my Peace Rose," Aubrey interrupted.

Douglas rescued the small rose stem and returned it to the counter. "She has taken this cutting from the rose bush in hopes it will develop a root," he explained to Kimberly's wonderment. "Sometimes it works; sometimes it doesn't, according to the green thumb gardeners. If it does, this little stalk will become a rose bush.

"It's never worked for you, has it?" Douglas added, turning toward Aubrey.

"Never." Aubrey solemnly shook her head.

"Sam Wade said to tell you that he would check with you later. They have arranged to have an officer stay with you tonight," reading from a yellow sheet that he had folded in half, Douglas listed the calls he had taken; "Barbara called, she must listen to the police scanner, sends her love and will call back. We're going to get going, if you think you'll be okay?"

"Of course, go. I'll be fine." Aubrey thanked Kimberly and Douglas. As though a curtain had opened onto a stage, she watched as Douglas and Kimberly set about, collecting Kimberly's purse and things Eric might want to take to their house. She was a voyeur; but not envying, not jealous, not particularly sad. Her myopic husband, rather ex-husband, still held claim to a part of her heart, a part like that reserved for a childhood friend one outgrows when there is nothing left in common except distant, sweet memories.

"Sure you don't want to stay for dinner?" Aubrey asked. Both Douglas and Kimberly insisted the afternoon had been too eventful, and Aubrey needed to relax. "Maybe another time," Douglas said.

"Another time would be good," Aubrey agreed.

Eric hesitated at the door, staring at his mother. "Are you sure?" he asked, shoulders square.

"I'm sure. Plus tomorrow is the first day you can sleep in, no school. You know how fast Detective Wade and all those cops got here this afternoon. He's already said that he will stop by to check on me. Besides, do you think this officer will allow anyone into the house, or anywhere near?" Aubrey nodded toward the uniformed policeman standing guard at the door. She hugged her son, and stood aside as the policeman unlocked the door for Douglas, Kim, and Eric to leave.

Having an officer stand watch through the night comforted her. Even though the guy had been caught and any others who might be connected would likely distance themselves from the entire situation, Aubrey was relieved the police department had taken precautions.

Chapter Forty-Two

The sky darkened as clouds thundered past the sun. It had been unusually hot all day. Warm air stirred and started to gust as huge rain drops splatted on the parched ground. The officer reached to open the front door for Detective Wade when loud banging noises startled Aubrey, reminding her of gunfire. Ice balls the size of moth balls tore holes in the leaves on the trees and shrubs as they plummeted toward the ground. Steam rose from the accumulated hail on the hot pavement. The horizon glowed an eerie pink-gray color. Detective Wade leapt across the threshold to safety from the storm. The hammering on the roof slowed. Within minutes, the sky cleared and the temperature moderated. The hail storm stopped as abruptly as it had started.

Aubrey blushed when Detective Wade praised her skills as a marksman.

"Do you have any idea yet who he is?" Aubrey asked.

"They haven't made a positive identification; you know, name, address, anything like that. But there's enough evidence to confirm he wasn't in this alone.

"Dr. Palmer is at the station now." Then, choosing his words carefully, he added, "It's been said he is making a voluntary statement. The picture of the van leaving the Pate property directly behind his car confirmed your suspicions that the events on

Thursday night at the hospital and the disappearance of Mrs. Owens and Dr. Pate might be related."

"I'm relieved to hear that," Aubrey said, grateful for the validation. "I felt like no one was taking me seriously. What I witnessed had to have been the harvest and pick up of organs, organs taken from the young man who died in the operating room that same night. I didn't want to believe a person as dear as Mary Beth could be associated with any sort of criminal activity; I still have a problem with that," she said as her voice quaked. "I figure Dr. Palmer had to be the leader. Something must have gone wrong. Or," she continued, as though speaking to herself, "Mary Beth and Ramsey were forced to participate. Whatever their reasons or rationale for it, they did it and now we have to find out what happened to Mary Beth and Ramsey." Aubrey had refused to allow herself to think the obvious.

To the rest of the world Mary Beth and Ramsey were the victims of a fire. Aubrey rationalized differently. They had been murdered and the same people had intended to kill her, probably because she had seen the van at the hospital. The information about the security camera posted at the entrance of Ramsey's drive had to make those involved realize she was a threat to their scheme to cover up the killings by destroying the house. Also, the car she had seen at the hospital the beginning of the week had to have been following her. Her paranoia was founded. It was the same car the wrecker pulled out of her driveway earlier as she heard Malcolm barking like crazy. In fact, she was surprised Mrs. Leland hadn't been over to check out the commotion. The hail storm likely drove her inside. When she found out all that had gone on today, she would appoint herself guardian of Aubrey and set up a command post right there at the kitchen table.

Detective Wade interrupted her thoughts. "It's not that we didn't take you seriously, but we are bound to follow procedure. We can't make accusations until we have some solid evidence. Your tenacity did cause us to dig deeper. Because of your statement, we covered territory we might not have considered. Thanks to you, there was no time for the dust to settle on their tracks."

"This afternoon, a totally unrelated comment by one of the staff nurses caused me to do a little detective work. I found out the weight of the patient was four full pounds lighter when he was received at the mortuary than he had been for the previous eight days in the ICU. It might not seem like much, but, kidneys weigh about one pound each and a heart nearly as much. If they took the time to harvest the liver, the difference could have been more significant."

Detective Wade's eyes widened in mock surprise, "An expert marksman and a detective, I'm impressed." Before he could continue, the policeman who had been standing in the doorway interrupted them. "There's a little dog across the alley whining and yelping. Herb just made his cruise past the back and he said the little guy had been carrying on when he made his rounds an hour ago."

"That would be Malcolm, my neighbor, Mrs. Leland's little dog. He's usually at her feet. She might be in the house and talking to someone, but it's not like her to leave him outside for that long." Aubrey stood and followed the policeman and Detective Wade through the back door, into the garage and toward the alley.

Detective Wade grabbed Aubrey's arm with his left hand as the policeman checked around the corner toward the patio. Aubrey caught sight of Mrs. Leland's body, crumpled in her irises, not moving. The policeman spoke into his walkie talkie, and it squawked before someone responded to his call for emergency services. Aubrey felt Detective Wade's grip on her arm loosen and she pulled free, dashing toward Mrs. Leland. She leaned over and placed her fingers against the inside of Mrs. Leland's wrist. "She's alive, but barely," she said as she clutched the feeble, weathered hand. Her pulse felt faint and thready to Aubrey's anxious fingers.

Not a good sign. Her chest barely moved with each breath. Dried blood strained her forehead. The hair at the back of her head was still damp from the pop shower and hail. Blood covered the stone her head rested on and pooled, turning the ground a dark burgundy. Aubrey lifted Mrs. Leland's eye lids. The large pupils constricted to light, a relief to Aubrey.

"Mrs. Leland, it's me, Aubrey. You're going to be all right. Malcolm barked until we came over to find you. He's your little hero." Aubrey noticed her chest move a little more with each breath, or was it her hopeful imagination?

Within seconds of hearing the sirens, two paramedics jumped from the ambulance and ran into the backyard. Aubrey was ushered aside as the two of them commenced to examine Mrs. Leland and access an IV line at the same time they questioned Aubrey and the others. Aubrey told them the name of Mrs. Leland's primary physician and what little she knew of her health issues, which were few. She knew she had only one child, a son who lived in Denver. Mrs. Leland moaned slightly as the paramedics gently lifted her onto a gurney for transport to the hospital.

Aubrey insisted on following the ambulance to the hospital. "She has no family here and I don't want her to be frightened. The guy who broke into my house must have encountered her first. Also, did you see the way she was holding her knife? That little stainless steel paring knife is Mrs. Leland's all-purpose garden tool. She was holding it like she was about to jab someone." Aubrey made a fist with her right hand, drawing her elbow toward her chest and then pushing her fist forward and away from herself. Detective Wade and the officer had made notes about the position Mrs. Leland was found in and the officer had combed the stone path among the flowers for any evidence an intruder might leave.

Mrs. Leland lay quietly on the hospital bed, the prongs of the oxygen tubing disappearing into her nose. The huge white bandage, wrapped turban style around her head, had a small, faint stain of blood on her forehead. Aubrey stared down at her neighbor. IV lines coursed from a hanging bag of blood cells down to the catheter that had been inserted in her arm while she was still in her own backyard.

The emergency room doctor indicated she had probably suffered a heat stroke or heart attack before she had fallen. Aubrey didn't agree. Of course she was dehydrated, who wouldn't be after roasting in the hot West Texas sun all afternoon, but she was as healthy as a horse. A scan of her head had assured them there was no bleeding within the skull. The monitor above the bed gave a rhythmic beep as a green line marked each heartbeat with a sharp vertical line. Her vital signs were all within normal range according to the numbers displayed. Careful not to dislodge any lines, Aubrey leaned forward to speak, "Mrs. Leland, it's me, Aubrey. Can you hear me?" Mrs. Leland didn't move.

"Momma." She caught herself on the verge of saying, "Momma."

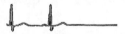

It hadn't been until Aubrey was in nursing school that she had known exactly how her mother had died. The term, "status asthmaticus," meant an acute asthma attack. Her mother had been dead on arrival at the hospital. She had died fighting for her breath.

Aubrey reached to adjust the oxygen tubing on Mrs. Leland's face.

Mrs. Leland moaned and tried to speak as she made an effort to turn her head to face Aubrey. Aubrey moved closer. "A man, tall, was in the alley. Up to no good." Her hand moved to grasp Aubrey's.

"It's okay. The police know all about it. You're safe now." Aubrey spontaneously bent and kissed Mrs. Leland on the cheek. "You don't have a thing to worry about. The doctor said you lost a little blood and got dehydrated; otherwise, they can't find a thing wrong with you. You'll be home in a couple of days. Malcolm will stay at the house with me."

She left her home number with the ICU nurses along with specific instructions to call anytime during the night if Mrs. Leland's condition should change for the worse.

Back at home, Aubrey collapsed on the sofa, exhausted after the most eventful day she had ever endured. She and Detective Wade sat silently for a few minutes, listening to the sound of the coffee maker. Detective Wade spoke first. "We didn't want to tire Mrs. Leland, but from what she was able to tell us, her attacker is the same guy who came after you. The doctor in the Emergency Room has stabilized him for transport to San Jacinto. He said the guy is sedated. Maybe we'll be allowed to question him in a couple of days."

Aubrey already had her own opinion of who was responsible and it was the stealthy harvesters, of which this guy was one. Whether Dr. Palmer had known about the attack on her or had been involved in any way wasn't an issue for her. The fact the murderous goon had been exposed and arrested and the exposure of Dr. Palmer for his deceptive practice put her at ease. Even if it did mean Blakely Hospital would be in the news. Why Rebecca had reacted the way she had earlier bothered Aubrey. For some reason Rebecca had resented Detective Wade's presence at the hospital.

"Do you remember the OR Director, Rebecca Krantz?" Aubrey asked.

Detective Wade nodded in acknowledgment.

"She came to my office this afternoon. I was astonished when she suggested you might be bothering me. I explained you seemed to have a genuine concern for solving the case. My mention of the notion Mary Beth and Ramsey were murdered caused her to turn ballistic on me. Her behavior this afternoon was as close as I've ever seen her come to losing it. In fact, she appeared frightened. It didn't last more than a few seconds, but I noticed a definite fear in her eyes. Enough to scare me. She bounced back to her old self in an instant. I lied, telling her she was probably right, in an attempt to smooth things over with her. For some reason she wants this whole thing to disappear.

"The only other time I have ever seen her show emotion that extreme was not long after Dr. Murphy, her boyfriend, had a stroke. Someone in the department made a scathing remark about the incident, saying the unit must be cursed after what happened to Dr. Crawford. Dr. Crawford was an internist at Blakely. It's been a year or two now, but her body was found in one of the OR rooms early one morning. The internal investigation determined she had been the victim of an unfortunate accident, a drug overdose after an argument with her significant other. Rebecca took on the same expression I saw today as she did when she told the person not to mention anything of the sort again."

Detective Wade stared curiously at Aubrey. She went on to explain. "Anyway, her boyfriend, Dr. Murphy, had a blood pressure crisis and ended up with a stroke that left him paralyzed on one side and unable to talk. They were at Rebecca's house when it happened. He didn't have a history of any health problems. He lives in a nursing home now. In fact the vacancy created by Dr. Murphy's forced resignation was filled by Dr. Palmer. Rebecca has never dated anyone else. Dr. Murphy was the love of her life. Her emotions were still raw. I'm sure Rebecca lashed out then because she thought she was protecting him. I don't know what caused the rage today. Maybe it's the threat of gossip among the staff in the hospital. Her life revolves around Blakely."

Detective Wade wondered if Rebecca Krantz might be the contact inside the hospital. Without displaying so much interest in Ms. Krantz, he probed. "Does Ms. Krantz get along well with Dr. Murphy's replacement, Dr. Palmer, or does he rub her the wrong way?"

"She chaired the committee that interviewed him for the position. As for liking him, no one would know. Rebecca has a reputation of running the department without allowing her personal interest to affect her professional judgment. That's exactly why I was so startled this afternoon. She was noticeably shaken." Aubrey pulled her cupped hands together, encircling the air, and frowned at the notion of herself becoming so extremely skeptical when it came to situations surrounding those she had known and trusted for years.

"Then she was probably relieved when Detective Stokes couldn't keep his appointment with her this afternoon," Detective Wade said. Then, pointing to his watch, he added, "It's getting late, I better get a move on."

"Thank you, Detective Wade," Aubrey said, feeling the inadequacy of the words, yet unable to utter more.

"Please, call me Sam," he said as he turned back toward her.

"Okay, Sam. Thanks."

Aubrey excused herself and retreated to the privacy of her bedroom. She heard Detective Wade give further instructions to the officer in charge of protecting her.

She woke, crosswise in the bed, after only three hours of fitful sleep. Lying in bed, replaying the scene of Rebecca and herself over and over in her head, a nurse's casual, sarcastic observation during a unit meeting more than a year before came to her mind.

All staff members had been encouraged to suggest topics for Quality Improvement surveys. The topics considered were either opportunities for improvement in patient care, or ways to better utilize resources. As Aubrey remembered, the nurse had said, "Dr. Murphy has a lousy record with his trachs. All of them die during the procedure. It's not an issue for our unit, but someone should pick up on a track record with outcomes like his. There certainly has to be room in his practice for improvement." The comment was taken in jest, since Rebecca reviewed all cases in the operating rooms with untoward outcomes and it was generally accepted if something happened in her department she would be the first to rectify it. Since his practice ended abruptly, it never became an issue. Until now. Aubrey intended to find out more about Dr. Murphy's trach patients. She especially wanted to know if they could have been the victims of unauthorized harvests.

Chapter Forty-Three

Aubrey arrived at the hospital well before six o'clock, followed by the officer assigned to protect her. First cases for the operating rooms were posted for seven thirty. The OR crew generally arrived at six thirty. The chilled silence of the locker room caused Aubrey to hurriedly change into her scrubs, and she grabbed a set for the officer who waited in the hall. She handed the scrubs to him, "You can slip these on over your uniform."

"I should check in at the station about this," the officer said.

"You are assigned to protect me. You have to protect me while I work. Everyone here wears scrubs. It's one of the rules."

Without further argument, the officer pulled the scrubs on over his uniform and followed Aubrey to the ICU. She purposefully neglected to explain to the officer what she was about to do was not a part of her routine at the hospital.

The admission log for the ICU had been documented exclusively on the computer for several months; however, prior to paperless system, the unit utilized the same type log books for entering admissions as the PACU used. The previous years' logs were kept on a shelf in the medicine room. Aubrey pulled out the ragged log books that contained ICU records for the previous two years. She scanned the long rows of admissions, focusing on the comment area in the far right column. If a patient expired in the ICU, the date and cause of death were documented in red ink. At the sight of any red ink notation, she read the diagnosis on admission and the patient's age. She wrote the medical record numbers of four patients on a piece of note paper. Four healthy young adults had met with untimely accidents, rendering them brain-dead and ultimately costing them their lives. Comments, noted in red ink, indicated all four had expired during surgery. The officer helped her to replace the log books.

No one was at the front desk of the Medical Records Department. She called out for assistance. When a young woman appeared from the back, Aubrey apologized for bothering her so early, "I want to get all my paperwork finished before my day gets too hectic." She handed her the numbers and asked, "Could you pull these charts for me, please?"

"No problem," the young woman said and took the list, disappearing into the expansive area of charts contained in sliding shelves that extended from the floor to the ceiling.

It didn't take long for her to have the data she needed. Aubrey made notes from each of the charts. It was incredible. Four patients. Three times the family member or the significant other had declined to donate the organs of their loved ones. Dr. Murphy had been consulted for surgery on all three of these patients. All three brain-dead patients were pronounced dead immediately after they had gone to the Operating Room to be trached and all three bodies were sent to the mortuary for cremation.

Aubrey and her shadow took the stairs to the third floor. From her office, she called Detective Wade at home. The officer gave a look of surprise when she said, "Good morning, Detective Wade. I'm at the hospital and I have some information that you might want to take a look at."

Entering the hospital, Rebecca paused, somewhat taken aback by the figure at the other end of the hall as it disappeared into the stairwell. She stopped at Medical Records. One glance at the log proved she had not been mistaken. Aubrey had arrived very early.

"May I help you, Ms. Krantz?"

"Yes, as a matter of fact, the same thing Aubrey wanted. Apparently our data collection sheet didn't include all the information we needed."

"No problem. At least she doesn't wait until the last day of the quarter, then come down here frantic for thirty charts she needs to audit. Here you go." She handed the four charts to Rebecca.

The names of the patients were on the tab beside the medical record number. Rebecca immediately recognized the names of three of the patients. She feigned a search through the charts for a few minutes as she mentally reviewed her next steps.

She changed into scrubs and filled her coffee mug as usual. In the anesthesia workroom, Rebecca took a small bottle from the refrigerator, swabbed the rubber seal and transferred the contents of the bottle into a syringe, which she tucked into the pocket of her blue scrub jacket. Safely in her office before she could be noticed, she closed the door and pushed the button in the center of the door knob, locking the door.

She sat at her desk and reached into the bottom left drawer for a plastic bag. The bag contained a tourniquet, alcohol swabs, a syringe with needle, an ampule of Sufenta, and an unopened vial of Versed. She pulled the syringe of succinylcholine from her pocket and laid it beside the other things. Fumbling with the back of the telephone until her hand found the cord, she unplugged it. From the same desk drawer, she retrieved a sealed envelope and positioned it against her nameplate. Everything was ready.

Sipping her coffee, she sat and waited. It was crucial she remain calm. There was no need to rush. In a half hour the OR staff would begin arriving. By the time they discovered what had happened and forced their way into the office, she would be free.

Rebecca stared at the envelope, her thoughts winding back to the night Dr. Crawford had come to her office.

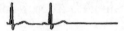

"So, you are the workaholic everyone says you are." Dr. Crawford had said as she leaned into Rebecca's office.

"Working on the budget while it's quiet," Rebecca lied. She had assisted Lance with a harvest and he would be walking into the office at any moment. "What are you doing here so late?" Rebecca stammered.

"Jan and I had a huge fight. I came back here to get away for awhile, give her time to cool down. I never expected to see anyone. I saw your light on and, as I was coming down the hall, I thought I saw a courier or somebody going toward the back elevator. It wasn't security; the guy was in plain clothes."

Lance had heard their conversation from the hall. He greeted the women heartily. When Dr. Crawford wilted in his embrace, Rebecca's eyes had widened in surprise.

Soon after Dr. Crawford's death, Rebecca made her own plan.

While waiting for Detective Wade, Aubrey busied herself detailing on paper the information she had discovered. She slammed the pencil down onto the papers.

"I need another peek at those charts. I failed to look at the anesthesia and circulating records. If we rush, they may not be re-shelved. It'll only take a minute." Aubrey and the officer again took the stairs to the first floor.

The door from the stairwell opened almost directly across from the entry to the Medical Records Department. "I reviewed several charts earlier. May I see them again?" Aubrey asked as she handed the clerk the list.

"Those are hot items this morning. Ms. Krantz just looked at them. She said something about needing more data from them."

Aubrey hoped her surprise at this news wasn't evident to the clerk. She read her badge, "Thank you, Jan. Maybe she got the information I need. I'll dash up and check. If she didn't, I will be back."

"Your list," the clerk called out, handing the list of patient names and chart numbers back to Aubrey.

Aubrey turned and led the way through the door. Inside the privacy of the stairwell, she turned to the officer and said, "Rebecca knows what I'm doing. We have to get upstairs." As she crammed the list into her pocket, a pink sticky note dislodged from the paper and landed in the bottom of her pocket.

The door to Rebecca's office was locked. Her locker was padlocked, but her street shoes were on the shoe rack. She was nowhere to be found. They were back in the hall before Aubrey spoke, "She has to be in her office." She raced to the phone and paged security.

They pounded on the door and tried, to no avail, to turn the knob. A dull thud could be heard from the other side of the door as the security guards forced the door open. With her arms folded in her lap, she sat slumped over the desk, her hair falling over the edge of her coffee mug. Aubrey instinctively reached for her wrist to check her pulse. Rebecca's clenched right hand held an empty syringe. The needle of the syringe was buried in a vein on the back of her left arm. A blank, sealed envelope sat, propped on the desk; Aubrey picked the letter up, grasping only the corner, and handed it to the police officer."

Aubrey gently cradled Rebecca's head in her arms and brushed the hair from across her face. Wide open eyes, frozen in a frightened stare, met Aubrey's desperate gaze. "It's okay. I'm right here with you and everything is fine," she said softly into Rebecca's ear as the tears streamed from her own eyes. She rocked and soothed her as Rebecca's lips parted, and her mouth gaped open, the last, shallow, labored exhalation trapped in her throat. Her expression softened and her muscles relaxed as her eyes locked on Aubrey's face.

The officer posted himself in the doorway, between Aubrey and the security guards. They honored Aubrey's plea as she gave them a hand signal to stay out. "There's nothing we can do for her," she said. Detective Wade appeared behind the guards. Their eyes met as she hugged the lifeless body against her chest. "Would you find Dr. Vincent? He's usually in the hospital by now. Check in the Men's Lounge."

Detective Wade returned with a tall, trim mountain of a man wearing dress trousers, his tie loosened and his shirt tail out. "Dr. Vincent, I need you," Aubrey spoke in a trembly voice. He had an innate sixth sense of always knowing the right thing to do and kindness flowed from him as naturally as blood flows through one's veins. As if he read her mind, Dr. Vincent wrapped the two women in his generous arms, his broad shoulders shielding them from the eyes of the world.

"I couldn't palpate a radial pulse. Her respirations were agonal. She would not have wanted any heroics. I didn't call a code, Dr. Vincent. I couldn't."

Chapter Forty-Four

Wind whipped around the cabin with a vengeance, as it sculpted the snow at the base of the stand of spruce trees lining the path to the garage into sharp drapes of crystal white. The late, May storm had pounded the area with cold. His breath made a white vapor as he exhaled. He removed his right glove and extracted the key from the pocket of his parka, the key with the string and vinyl coated label marked '108 Duncan Ridge'. The key turned the deadbolt. One push of the heavy cedar door and, as the hinges squeaked in objection, Vince squinted to take a look at his new home.

Bought sight unseen from an absentee owner self described as 'not as outdoorsy as I thought I was', the cabin was everything the advertisement had described. A stone fireplace was centered on the north wall. Framing the fireplace, floor to ceiling bookcases covered the remainder of the living room wall. A long overstuffed sofa sat facing the fireplace with throw pillows depicting a fly fisher tying a colorful tie onto his line, casting into a mountain stream, and posing with an open creel containing his fresh catch. Two huge chairs, covered in the same olive color leather as the sofa, flanked the sofa. The wide planked wood floor was stained a light honey color. An open stairway led to the sleeping loft. The seller told Vince the wood used to build the cabin had been harvested on site and the original owner had milled and planed all the wood for the cabinets and bookcases with his own hands.

The kitchen had another, smaller fireplace beside the conventional cooking range. A short hall separating the kitchen and living room led to the bathroom. A huge walk-in closet was situated by the back entry. By instruction of the seller, Vince found a folder behind the top shelf of the closet with another set of keys, operation manuals and warranty papers on all the appliances, generator and tractor, and a diagram of the cabin. This detailed drawing showed a basement. The seller had not mentioned a basement. After studying the diagram, Vince slid the bench from its position against a wall underneath a row of pegs for coats and hats to an open area between shelves and a space for hanging clothes. Then he rolled the rug back to find the trap door. He reached inside the basement for the light switch and flipped it to find a small fortress. Shelves containing canned foods, candles, a first aid kit, blankets, garden tools, and camping gear lined the perimeter. A column about five foot square in the center reached from the floor to the ceiling. It looked like an elevator shaft. A heavy door was on one side. All the water pipes were contained inside this core basement.

He remembered Mitchell using the corny line about being pioneers. Vince was the pioneer, a new man with a new name and a new home, time to shed his past.

On Thursday he looked out the upstairs window to see the shadow of someone standing on the far side of the row of spruce trees. His eyes followed the drive back toward the road. No evidence of a vehicle or of foot traffic could be seen. Several inches of new fallen snow were undisturbed. The shadow moved side to side.

Vince slipped on his trousers and flannel shirt and went downstairs. The shadow had moved. He couldn't see it. A noise at the back door gave him a start. Vince eased toward the back hall. He stopped at the closet and pulled a rifle off the rack. He pushed the cartridge into place and took aim before he shouted, "Who is it?"

Exhaling slowly, he released the hammer and engaged the safety. "Dillon, I'm glad you remembered."

Chapter Forty-Five

As she leaned to pull a spent bloom from her Peace Rose, Aubrey's neck beaded with perspiration under the blazing mid-morning sun. The red dry earth had cracked for want of rain leaving the pale, straw-colored roots of the grass exposed. City regulations mandated sprinklers only be used between the hours of seven and ten in the evening. Residents whose house numbers were even numbers could water on even numbered days of the month and the houses on the opposite side of the street were allowed to water on odd numbered days. A water shortage existed, as it usually did in West Texas during the middle of summer.

She picked up the gallon-sized plastic ice cream buckets she had used to bring the gray water she collected from the washing machine in the basement to water her roses and trees. Drought wasn't going to claim them if she could prevent it. While putting the buckets away, she heard a car stop at the front of the house. The events of the previous week caused her to view everything with a cautionary eye, abandoning her blind trust. A change in character she acknowledged with ambiguity. She leaned forward to peer out the basement window. A pair of black cowboy boots with faded jeans pushed down over them stepped up onto the walk near the front door.

When she arrived upstairs and opened the door, Detective Wade stood on the front step, his hand poised to ring the bell.

"Good morning. You're out early for a Saturday. I hope you are not going to ask me to give another deposition."

"I wouldn't put you through that again. Actually, I received an early morning wake up call." He continued as he followed her toward the den. "Those federal boys in San Jacinto don't take the time to sleep. Jon's down there following them around for the weekend. If I don't watch out I'll lose my sidekick."

Sitting opposite her, Detective Wade disclosed the reason for his unannounced visit. "It seems the letter Ms. Krantz left on her desk has kept them busy."

The letter Aubrey had found on Rebecca's desk had been written as a confessional letter, listing names of contacts. As a result of the letter a string of arrests had been made. Those apprehended were part of an international group associated with the unauthorized harvest of human organs from brain-dead patients and the disappearance and murder of healthy young people for their organs. This group had also been responsible for soliciting doctors and hospital employees into their secret labyrinth. Thanks, for the most part to Rebecca, their malignant ventures had been shut down.

"Rebecca Krantz and Dr. Lance Murphy became involved in the group after they had been on vacation in Mexico. One of their contacts was the service manager at the Mercedes-Benz dealership.

He tried to fly the coop, but the feds caught him. The van driver, the guy you saw at the hospital, hasn't been located. Odds are he won't.

"When Dr. Murphy couldn't practice anymore, because of his stroke, the group wanted to insure his replacement would want to work with them. Dr. Palmer was the hungry new doctor who fit the bill. He could step right into Dr. Murphy's shoes. Palmer hasn't admitted any knowledge of Ms. Krantz's involvement."

Detective Wade's voice softened as he continued, "I reckon you know what I'm going to tell you about your nurse friend and her fiancé. According to the statement of one of the people in the group, they were alive when they were taken out of the country."

Aubrey nervously repositioned herself on the sofa and faced Detective Wade with her eyes wide open, bracing herself for the inevitable.

"Most likely, they never regained consciousness," he said and came to sit beside Aubrey on the sofa. "Their paper trail is purposefully sketchy, but by all indications their organs were harvested and sold on the black market." He paused, watching as Aubrey gazed out the window, her hands nervously fiddling with a piece of fishing line.

She collected strength to speak, "At a nursing conference, we had a guest lecturer who spoke to us about heart transplants. This was several years ago, when the procedure was relatively new. The heart muscle itself never feels pain after a transplant. The nerve is severed when the heart is harvested. I remember thinking how odd that must be; to know your heart couldn't feel. The emotional engine of the body gets disconnected." She pulled the string's ends, dislodging the knot.

Aubrey could recall, as though it were yesterday, the leap of warmth that filled her heart when Eric had been born, also, the squeezing pressure of her aching heart when Douglas had moved out, and, just days earlier, the bolt of power that surged through her heart when she had so narrowly escaped death.

"To me, life is interpreted through the heart. Greg Palmer and those goons robbed Mary Beth and Ramsey, made them sacrificial donors. They murdered them.

"Their hearts, lungs, kidneys, livers and, for that matter, tissue, bones, all were sold to make someone rich. Sure others lived, but they couldn't possibly care to have life restored at that price. To think the vile, vile creeps who did this were justifying their deeds by telling themselves they were helping others; it's like a religious lunatic that quotes the one bit of scripture that he thinks justifies his behavior."

Aubrey agreed with the premise if a person had no chance of survival and his organs could save another's life or several others' lives, then it would be the most generous thing one could do. However, it was a personal decision made by the person or his closest family member, not a third party, especially not one with money to gain. To do otherwise was illegal, immoral, unethical, and absolutely horrific.

"Is Greg Palmer locked up?" she wanted to know.

"He has been released on bail; the state medical board will have a go at him now. It's possible he'll never practice medicine again. Still claims he didn't know Mrs. Owens and Dr. Pate were going to die."

"Have the families been told?"

"They have," Detective Wade said, nodding. "Mr. Pate took the news surprisingly well and so did Mrs. Owens's family. I think they're relieved to be through with it."

Detective Wade sat with the tip of his thumb against his bottom lip wishing for something clever to say that would lighten the lines on Aubrey's face or console her. After a few minutes of awkward silence, he stretched his legs out in front of himself and settled back against the cushions. He wrapped his arm around her shoulders and pulled her close. Aubrey's tears, making darker blue dots on his pale blue shirt, fell without hesitation, as they sat together in silence.

Chapter Forty-Six

Aubrey squinted, adjusting her eyes to the near darkness as she entered the softly lit chapel. People wearing somber faces filled the dark wooden pews. Celtic music drifted from the corners of the room, filling the awkward gaps of silence between the whispered comments of the mourners. The wide planked wooden floor groaned in mournful sighs as friends filed past the front pew to offer their condolences to the senior Mr. Pate and the family of Mary Beth Owens. Centered on the table at the altar, a portrait of Ramsey and Mary Beth stood flanked by grand bouquets of white and yellow roses. Bluebonnets blanketed the outer walls near the altar.

As friends and relatives opened the door at the back of the chapel to enter, a shaft of light flooded the altar area reflecting on the picture of the couple who had been robbed of this sunny day.

Aubrey couldn't remember ever having attended a memorial service for anyone in the chapel at Blakely. The hospital chaplain generally officiated over a non-denominational worship service weekday mornings and on Sundays, and the chapel remained open all hours for anyone who wanted to enter to pray or meditate.

Once a year, during Nurses Week, this was the site for a blessing of the hands service. Aubrey had been especially moved by the ceremony the previous year, when she had had the opportunity to attend with Mary Beth. Two chaplains had been stationed at the altar. One offered a prayer of blessing, as she symbolically lifted water from the basin into her cupped hands and covered the nurse's hands with this water. The second chaplain prayed for strength and wisdom for the nurse and thankfulness for the service the nurse provided, as she methodically dried the nurse's hands, starting with the fifth fingers on each hand and moving toward the thumbs. It had been the end of the day and the only light in the chapel had been the soft glow of the candles.

That same atmosphere of calm and peacefulness, combined with the soothing music, prevailed today. A welcome solace after the nightmare of activity over the past weeks.

Aubrey cleared her throat and straightened in the pew where she sat with several friends from the hospital. To distract herself from looking at the portrait, she focused on a stained glass window depicting a lamb in a green pasture and marveled at the halo of light shining around the lamb's wooly off-white coat. She crossed her hands over her heart and prayed.

As the time neared for the memorial service to begin, the last of those standing found seats toward the rear of the chapel where only a few empty seats remained. The Celtic music stopped and the organist began to play "Amazing Grace." The door at the back creaked as it was pushed open. Again, light flooded the altar. Aubrey noticed people turn to stare at the person entering the chapel. There were hushed whispers as a slender woman dressed in a straight, knee length, long sleeve black dress walked down the center aisle then bent, kissing Mr. Pate on the cheek. Mr. Pate leapt from

B J Gupton

the pew and with a trembling hand, grasped the hand of the woman and drew her close to himself and held her in a tender embrace as everyone in the chapel watched.

He turned back toward the pew and motioned for the lady to take a seat beside him. As the lady turned to sit, Aubrey recognized her; as did practically everyone in the chapel. Aubrey had not seen Margaret Pate since she and Ramsey had divorced, and she had moved away; however, there was no mistaking this beautiful pale ivory skinned woman, with red wavy hair pulled back in a knot at the nape of her neck in an attempt to control the locks, was in fact the former wife of Ramsey Pate. She had driven from New Mexico for the memorial service. Eyes shifted to avoid staring, as the organist pressed out the last chords of music and the chaplain took his place behind the altar.

Meanwhile, Detective Wade stumbled past several people, mumbling apologies as he stepped over their feet, to squeeze into the pew beside Aubrey. He leaned down and brushed her cheek with his lips.

"Hi Sam," she whispered. Aubrey allowed herself to settle against the strength of his shoulder. After the organist had struck the last cord, a very faint lub-dub seemed to echo in Aubrey's ear.

Follow me on Facebook at:
Brenda Joyce Gupton

Contact me at: bj.gupton@yahoo.com

CPSIA information can be obtained at www.ICGtesting.com
Printed in the USA
LVOW06s1820030914

402284LV00001B/2/P